Brave Music

of a

Distant Drum

Brave Music of a Distant Drum

MANU HERBSTEIN

Red Deer PRESS

Published by Red Deer Press, A Fitzhenry & Whiteside Company
195 Allstate Parkway, Markham, ON, L3R 4T8
www.reddeerpress.com

Published in the United States by Red Deer Press, A Fitzhenry & Whiteside Company
311 Washington Street, Brighton, Massachusetts, 02135

Edited for the Press by Kathy Stinson
Cover and text design by Daniel Choi
Cover Images Courtesy of Shutterstock and iStockphoto.

Printed and bound in Canada

5 4 3 2 1

We acknowledge with thanks the Canada Council for the Arts, and the Ontario Arts Council for their support of our publishing program. We acknowledge the financial support of the Government of Canada through the Canada Book Fund for our publishing activities.

ONTARIO ARTS COUNCIL
CONSEIL DES ARTS DE L'ONTARIO

Canada Council for the Arts
Conseil des Arts du Canada

Library and Archives Canada Cataloguing in Publication
Herbstein, Manu
Brave music of a distant drum / Manu Herbstein.
ISBN 978-0-88995-470-0
I. Title.
PR9379.9.H47B73 2011 j823'.92 C2011-905856-1

Publisher Cataloging-in-Publication Data (U.S)
Herbstein, Manu
Brave Music of a Distant Drum / Manu Herbstein.
[192] p. : cm.
Summary: The story of an African woman enslaved in Brazil who summons her son to come and write down her story so that her granddaughter and her granddaughter's children can one day read it and know their history.
ISBN: 978-0-88995-470-0 (pbk.)

Back cover image, left: Plan showing the typical storage of captured Africans aboard a regulated slave ship bound for the Americas. Courtesy of Library of Congress Prints and Photographs division, digital ID cph.3a34658 PD-US.

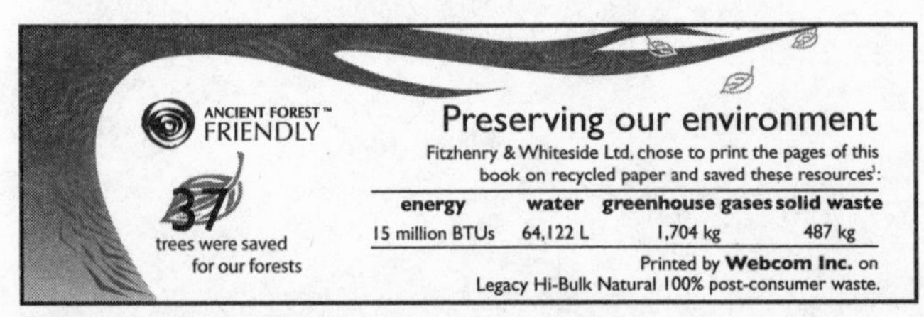

MIX
Paper from responsible sources
FSC® C004071

[1]Estimates were made using the Environmental Defense Paper Calculator.

for Marie Helene, Sophie Akosua and Kwaku Thamsanqa

Contents

A Note from the Author

A good story must speak for itself, and I expect every reader to find something different in Ama's story and Kwame's. All the same, a brief sketch of the historical background might serve to set *Brave Music of a Distant Drum* within the context of our times.

The European voyages of discovery in the fifteenth century ushered in modern Western society. The trans-Atlantic slave trade started shortly after these initial voyages. The slave plantations in the Americas were testing grounds for the future factories of the industrial revolution and for the concentration camps established by the British in South Africa and by the Nazis in Europe in the Second World War.

Many years after the abolition of slavery, the scars of the slave trade survive. No one who lives on the Atlantic rim and in its hinterland is untouched by this history. Sadly, few of us know much about it. My friend Prof. Kwadwo Opoku-Agyemang addresses this issue in the introduction to his collection of poems, *Cape Coast Castle*:

> The effects of enslavement have lasted this long because of the silence that surrounds its history ... The power of the fetish of slavery is enhanced by keeping it hidden ... To dissolve the fetish it is necessary to keep the story of slavery and the slave trade open-ended and to avoid closure; to clear the way to debate and to perpetually initiate rather than conclude the argument so that every new generation may visit it to quarry its lessons.

My hope is that *Brave Music of a Distant Drum* will introduce a new generation of readers to this history and encourage them to broaden their knowledge of it.

About the title:

You will find the phrase "the brave music of a distant drum" in Edward Fitzgerald's translation of the ***Rubáiyát of Omar Khayyám***; but here, the brave music is Ama's story, and Kwame's, standing in perhaps for the lost stories of some of the twelve million Africans who were subjected to forced emigration across the ocean, and for the stories of their descendants and their struggle for freedom and dignity. Like the sound of a distant drum, this music reverberates over space and over time, echoing back and forth across the Atlantic and across the centuries.

Manu Herbstein

Characters

The principal characters are shown in bold type. An asterisk indicates an historical character.

AFRICA

FAMILY

Ama	the heroine, known as Nandzi in the earlier part of the story; later known as Pamela and as "One-Eye"
Nandzi	see Ama
Pamela	see Ama
"One-Eye"	see Ama
Nowu	Nandzi's four-year-old brother, son of Tabitsha and Tigen
Tabitsha	Nandzi's mother, Tigen's junior wife
Tigen	Nandzi's father, Tabitsha's husband
Sekwadzim	Tabitsha's father, Nandzi's maternal grandfather
Satila	Nandzi's betrothed
Itsho	Nandzi's lover

YENDI (Dagomba capital)	
Abdulai	commander of the Bedagbam slave raiders
Damba	Bedagbam slave raider
Suba	young boy, captured Bekpokpam slave
Koranten Péte*	Asante consul in Yendi, commander of the central division of the Asante army (1720?–1810?)
Akwasi Anoma	Asante official

KUMASE (Asante capital)	
Osei Kwadwo*	fourth Asantehene (king of Asante), ruled 1764–1777 (say: O-say Ko-jo)
Osei Kwame*	fifth Asantehene, ruled c 1777–1803 (see Kwame Panin)
Konadu Yaadom*	Asantehemaa (queen-mother of Asante), 1752?–1809; maternal aunt (or mother?) of Kwame Panin
Kwame Panin*	nephew (or son?) of Konadu Yaadom; the future Asantehene Osei Kwame
Konkonti*	Chief Executioner of Mampong
Mensa	Asante musketeer
Esi	female Asante pawn; friend of Ama

ELMINA

Esi	see above
Jensen	Danish Chief Merchant at Elmina Castle; second in command and successor to Pieter de Bruyn
Pieter de Bruyn	Director-General (Governor) of the Dutch West India Company at Elmina Castle; also known as Mijn Heer (say: de Brain)
Elizabeth de Bruyn	deceased wife of Pieter de Bruyn
Augusta	Fante trader in Edina (Elmina town); former wife of Pieter de Bruyn
Hendrik van Schalkwyk	Minister of the Dutch Reformed Church, Preacher and Chaplain of Elmina Castle (say: fun skulk-vake)
Rev. Philip Quaque*	chaplain at Cape Coast castle (say: Philip Kweku)
Rose*	Fante wife of Jensen
David Williams	Welsh captain of the English slave ship Love of Liberty
Richard Brew*	Irish slave trader; governor of Castle Brew at Anomabu

THE LOVE OF LIBERTY	
George Hatcher	seaman
Harry Baker	seaman
Joe Knox	seaman
Fred Knaggs	seaman
Butcher	surgeon
Gavin Williams	nephew of Captain David Williams; passenger; later British Consul in Salvador
Kofi	young Akan boy;
Kofi's mother	slave
Tomba	slave from the Upper Guinea coast; slave

AMERICA

SALVADOR	
Roberto	slave of Fante origin
Josef	slave at the Engenho de Cima; boatman

ENGENHO DE CIMA	
Fifi	Fante slave at the Engenho do Meio
The Senhor	owner (senhor de engenho) of the Engenho de Cima
The Senhora	wife of the Senhor
Jacinta	female slave without hands
Jesus Vasconcellos	General Manager
Father Isaac	Catholic chaplain
Alexandré	Mulatto son of the Senhor
Miranda	daughter of the Senhor and the Senhora
Bernardo	Fante slave; chief carpenter
Tomás	Hausa slave; blacksmith
Olukoya	Yoruba slave; slave driver
Ayodele	wife of Olukoya
Wono	Yoruba slave; wife of Josef
Benedito	old Crioulo slave; catechist
Pedro	slave; underdriver
João	Portuguese name of Tomba

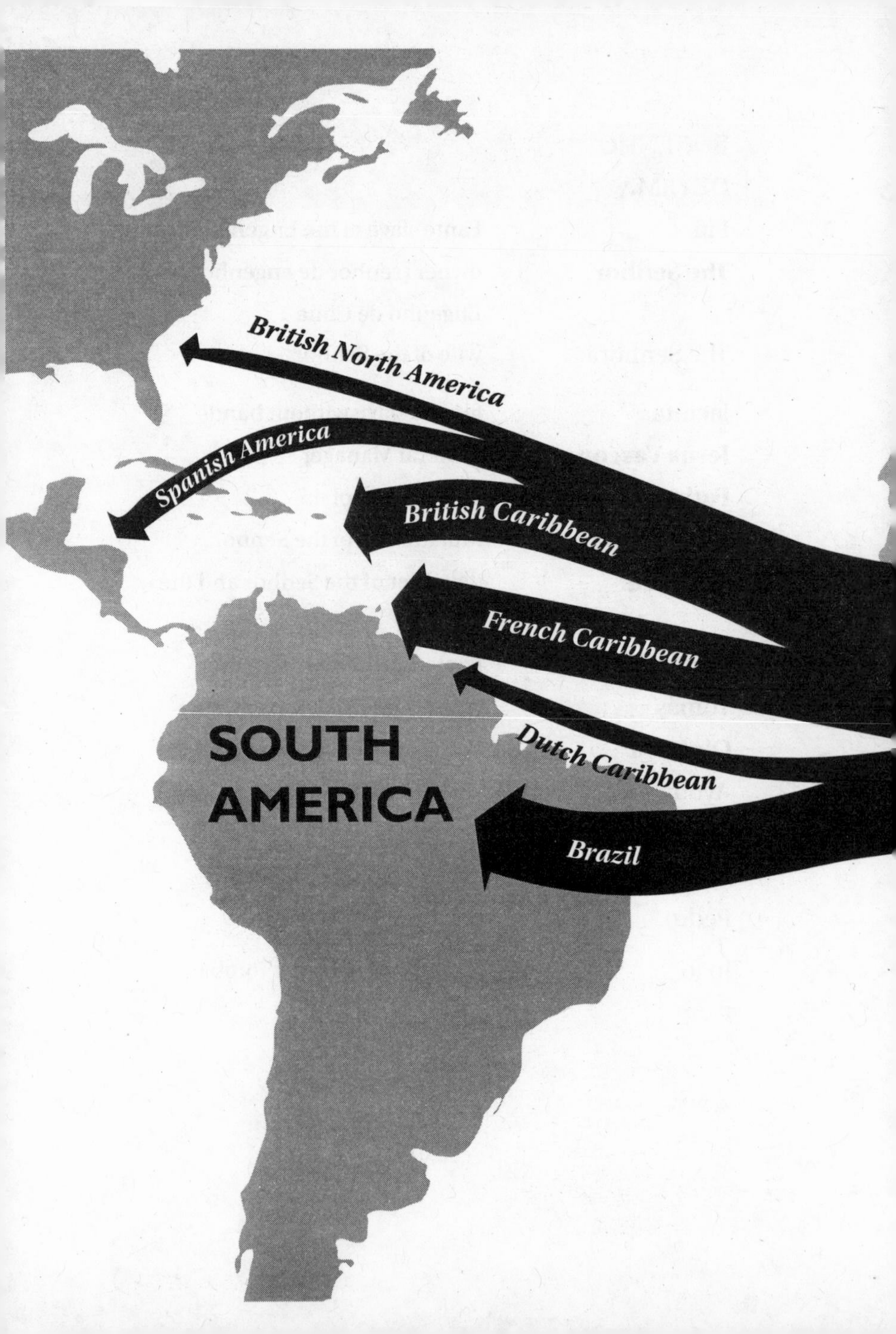
British North America
Spanish America
British Caribbean
French Caribbean
Dutch Caribbean
Brazil
SOUTH
AMERICA

The Atlantic Slave Trade Volume and Destinations 1701-1810

AFRICA

500,00
1,000,000
2,000,000
3,000,000
4,000,000
5,000,000
6,000,000

Volume

(after P.D. Curtin)

CHAPTER ONE

Ama

I am blind.

Knaggs' whip took out my right eye many years ago; and now my left eye, too, is only good for shedding tears. My hand can still hold a quill but, without guidance, the marks it makes are mere scribbles.

I have a story to tell. It lies within me, kicking like a child in the womb, a child whose time has come. If I had died last night, my story would by now be lying with me in my shallow grave; but I did not die last night and I will still tell my story. It is true that Wono and Ayodele have heard parts of it, and Olukoya and Josef, too, but though they are all still blessed with good eyesight, none of them can write, at least not well enough to be my scribe.

Tomba was my husband, father of our only child, Kwame. After Tomba's death, Miranda took Kwame away to the city. Her husband, Senhor Gavin Williams, is the

British Consul there. According to the laws of Brazil, I am Miranda's property. So is Kwame.

Now Kwame is a grown man with a wife and a child of his own. Today he will bring them to meet me for the first time. I must not think of it; it makes my heart pound in my chest. But I cannot control my thoughts any more than I can control the beating of my heart. My granddaughter Nandzi Ama, named after me, is two years old. I shall take her in my arms and hold her close to me.

I taught Kwame his letters and numbers. Miranda—and I bless her for this—let him share the lessons she gave to her daughter Elizabeth, who is just one week older than Kwame. She had to keep it secret, because it is against the laws of the Portuguese to teach slaves to read and write. When Kwame was grown, Miranda persuaded Senhor Gavin to give him employment as a clerk. Just think! He was still a small boy when he was taken from me, and now he is a man, and although like me, he is a slave, he gets paid for his work.

I pray that Kwame will bring ink and paper with him as I asked. Then I will tell him the story of my life, from the beginning; and Tomba's, such of it as I know; and he will write it all down. And one day Nandzi Ama will read it; and her children, too. Then they will know who their ancestors were and where they came from; and they will understand that the shame of their enslavement lies with the slave traders not with the enslaved.

Josef

She was sleeping when we arrived at the senzala, sitting on her low stool with her back against the wall, fast asleep. I put my hand on her shoulder and squeezed gently to wake her.

"Sister Ama," I told her in Fante (we always speak Fante when we are alone together), "he has arrived. Your son is here."

She was confused.

"I am sorry," I said. "You were dozing. I woke you."

She tried to get to her feet. I had to help her up.

Now they were standing face to face; but Sister Ama is blind and, of course, she couldn't see him. I sensed that she expected him to embrace her.

"Zacharias," I told him in Portuguese, "this is your mother, Sister Ama."

She started.

"Zacharias?" she asked. "Is it not Kwame? My son Kwame Zumbi?"

I tried to reassure her.

"Sister Ama," I told her, speaking again in Portuguese so that Zacharias could understand, "Senhora Miranda calls him Zacharias. You remember, that is the name he was given at his christening? That is what they call him in Salvador."

The chance for them to embrace one another had passed. Zacharias stood there, shifting from one foot to the other.

"Take my hand," she said.

He did as she asked. He still hadn't said a word.

"Let me feel your face," she said.

Zacharias

My name is Zacharias Williams. I am employed as a clerk and scribe by Senhor Gavin Williams, Consul of the United Kingdom of Great Britain and Ireland to the Portuguese Viceroyalty of Brazil in Salvador, Bahia.

Soon I will be a free man. Senhora Miranda has promised to give me my freedom, with a proper certificate of manumission to prove it.

Senhora Miranda is the wife of Senhor Gavin. She owns the sugar plantation and mill known as the Engenho de Cima. She inherited it from her father when he died.

That is where I am now.

Senhora Miranda says she was born here and lived here until she married Senhor Gavin. She tells me that I was born here, too, but that she took me away to Salvador when I was a small boy. I do not doubt her word but I remember nothing of this place. It is as if I have come here for the first time.

My mother, the slave woman Ama, lives here. She is old and blind and unwell and, I have to say it, ugly. I don't remember her at all. She is a stranger to me. Indeed, I wonder whether she really is my mother. How could a mother give up her only child, and to a white woman at that? There is something else I don't understand: she speaks good English, much better than Senhora Miranda does. Senhora Miranda speaks English with a strong accent. Senhor Gavin laughs at her English and that makes her angry. Senhora Miranda is a rich white lady. My mother is an old black slave, dressed in a torn, faded dress. Most slaves can't even speak good Portuguese. Yet my mother also speaks English almost as well as Senhor Gavin does. And he is an Englishman, a genuine white Englishman. My mother's perfect English is a mystery to me.

I don't know what to call my mother. If she were just another old African slave woman, I would call her by her name, Ama. But I cannot do that. If she is really my mother, I must treat her with respect. "Honor thy father and thy mother," it says in the Holy Bible. I think I shall call her My Mother.

My name, as I said, is Zacharias. But my mother refuses to use it. Senhora Miranda says that I was baptized with that name. She was my godmother and Senhor Gavin was my godfather. But my mother calls me Kwame. She says my name is Kwame Zumbi. That is not a Christian name. She says that that is the name my father gave me. I am on the point of asking her to tell me about my father but I am too shy.

She wants me to write down the story of her life as she dictates it to me. She says she should have written it herself before she lost her eyesight, but she was lazy and, what is more, she did not have ink and paper. Amazing. A ladina, an African-born slave, who says she can read and write. Who could have taught her? It is against the law to teach slaves to read and write. Senhor Gavin took a risk when he agreed to let Senhora Miranda teach me. But the Senhora insisted. She said that no one in Salvador would trouble the Consul of the English king. She was giving lessons to her own daughter Elizabeth, Senhorita Elizabeth, and she said she could not let me remain ignorant. She told him, "I owe it to Ama." I didn't understand what she meant. I still don't. Was she talking about my mother, Ama? What could Senhora Miranda owe to a poor old slave woman like my mother? I should not have come here. This place is full of mysteries, disturbing mysteries.

Josef brought the message. Josef is the old slave who takes messages and things between Salvador and the Engenho. He is a boatman. It was Josef who brought me here across the bay today. I didn't want to come, but he told Senhora Miranda that my mother had been ill. The Senhora crossed herself and said, "I would never forgive myself if Ama were to pass away without seeing Zacharias again." She said I should take my wife, Iphigenia, and our baby daughter

Carlota, but I told her that Carlota was too young to make the journey. She said I should stay here for a month.

Ama's story

We call my country Kekpokpam. It is in Africa; but when I lived there, "Africa" meant nothing to me. Kekpokpam lies many days walk from the sea, but when I lived there, I had never even heard of the sea.

Our home was a cluster of thatched round houses surrounded by a low wall. There were no other houses within sight of ours. My birth name is Nandzi. My father was called Tigen, though, out of respect, I never called him by his name. My mother Tabitsha was his junior wife. She had been married before, to my father's younger brother, but he had died. She had her own round house, a single room, and I slept there with her and my baby brother Nowu. My father Tigen must surely have joined the ancestors by now. But my mother might still be alive.

My father was rich. We had two cows, sheep and goats, as well as ducks, chicken, and guinea fowl. My father's farms were spread all around our house. There was plenty of land. He grew guinea corn and millet, yams, groundnuts, and rice. And he had a field of hunger rice, too, in case the grain in our silos did not last until the next harvest. My mother had her own small farm, where I helped her to grow tomatoes and red pepper. My father and my brothers would set traps in the river to catch fish. I was not allowed to eat meat (it is taboo for unmarried girls) but sometimes, when there was no one watching, my mother Tabitsha would let me have a taste.

Our language, Lekpokpam, was the only one I could speak or understand, except for the few words of Dagbani and Yoruba and Hausa I picked up in the market.

I was given in marriage soon after I was born. My husband was called Satila. Once a year he would bring bundles of guinea corn to my father to pay for my upkeep, one bundle the first year, two the second year, and so on. I hated him. He was old and ugly. I wanted to marry Itsho. Itsho was my lover. He was my own age. We used to go into the corn fields together, or to a secret pool near the river. Or if my father was away, my mother would leave us alone in her room.

It was my mother Tabitsha who broke the bad news to me. Satila had given notice to my father Tigen that he would soon bring the last sixteen bundles of guinea corn and take me away. I dreaded that day. Once I moved to Satila's home, I would be properly married and meeting Itsho would be out of the question.

Then the distant sound of drums told us that my mother's father, Sekwadzim, had died. I should have gone to the funeral, but my small brother Nowu was sick, and my mother Tabitsha said I should stay at home and look after him. I watched them until they were out of sight over the brow of the first hill. I felt lonely and scared. I had never been left all alone like that before.

Zacharias

She puts her hand on top of my head.

"You are taller than your father was," she says.

She runs her hands over my face, feeling my forehead, my eyebrows, my nose, my lips; and then my jacket, my shirt, my trousers. I am fortunate; my master's hand-me-downs fit me well. I sense her approval.

"Kwame," she says, "to me you will always be Kwame and that is what I shall call you. Kwame, where is your wife? And where is my granddaughter, whom you named after me?"

That is a surprise. I gave our daughter a Christian name. I called her Carlota, after the Princess of Brazil.

Josef catches my eye. He waves his index finger at me. I understand his silent message. He invented the story that I named our baby girl after my mother. He is warning me. He doesn't want me to tell her the truth.

"My Mother," I tell her, "your granddaughter had a fever and we didn't want to expose her to the journey across the bay. Iphigenia had to stay behind to look after her."

"Who is Iphigenia?" she asks.

"Iphigenia is my wife," I tell her.

Ama's story

There was a puff of dust on the horizon. I saw it but paid

no attention because I was carrying Nowu on my back and he was crying. I walked him up and down and comforted him with a lullaby. When he fell asleep, I put him down in my mother's room.

Itsho had brought us an antelope the day before. My mother Tabitsha had prepared some of the meat and was cooking it in a light soup. She had left for Sekwadzim's funeral in such a hurry that the pot was still simmering over its three stones. It smelled so good. I knew it was wrong, but what harm could come of one small sip, I asked myself. There was no one around to see me, to report me to my father for breaking the taboo. I tried the soup. It was delicious. Even today, as I recall the steamy bush-meat aroma of that antelope soup and the sharp taste of pepper on my tongue, I salivate. I filled a bowl and put it to my lips. As I did so, I felt the ground shake beneath my feet.

I dropped the bowl and the soup spilled onto the ground. I hardly had to look. I knew. That puff of dust had been made by a band of mounted Bedagbam raiders. All through my childhood I had heard stories about them. They had stolen our land; they were our enemies.

There was no time to escape. Had I tried, they would have seen me and caught me. And there was Nowu; I couldn't just leave him. I did the first thing that came into my mind. I entered my mother's room, lay down on the mat next to him, and pulled some skins over us. It was already getting to midday and it was hot. At once I began to sweat. I heard the snorting of the horses and strange voices. I lay quite still, listening to my heartbeat.

I heard them come into the room. Nowu sighed in his sleep. Afraid that he would wake up and cry out, I put my hand over his mouth, inadvertently waking him. He struggled to free himself. The Bedagbam must have seen the skins move. They ripped them off us.

I am not going to tell you what happened next. Just to think of it brings back the humiliation and pain as if it were yesterday. But this you should know: I did not give up without a fight. I bit the man's finger right down to the bone. I tasted his Bedagbam blood. He punished me for that. When he had finished with me, he took my cloth and tore a strip off it to use as a bandage. I still have that cloth. I have kept it all these years. It is the only memento I have of home.

I must have fainted. The next thing I remember is finding myself strapped across the back of a mule, my hands bound. I was crying and my nose was running. The animal's hooves threw up the red dust and it stuck to my face. I was desperately worried about Nowu. Put yourself in his position, just four years old, feverish, and left all alone. What's more, I was certain that my father, Tigen, would blame me for abandoning him.

A man I later learned was named Damba rode ahead with my animal and the other pack mules tied to his horse with leather straps. When we had traveled some distance, I raised my head. There was a man approaching us on foot from one side. As we came closer, I saw that it was Itsho. He must have been at the funeral and, seeing that I had been left at home, decided to come and visit me. I screamed to warn him.

He shouted, "Nandzi, is that you?"

I called back in our language. Damba couldn't understand what I was saying. He beat me with his fist and told me to shut my mouth. I could sense how nervous he was. The Bedagbam fear our men.

Damba was armed, but so was Itsho. Both had bows and spears. Itsho wanted to attack. I begged him to go and take care of Nowu and to wait until after dark before trying to rescue me. I knew that he would raise a force from amongst the young men at Sekwadzim's funeral.

CHAPTER TWO

Zacharias

She says she is tired. I am tired, too. There have been heavy rains, and the road from the bay up to the engenho is like a river of mud. It sticks to your feet. *Massapé,* Josef says they call it. Good for the sugar cane, he says, but not so good for walking.

She throws a threadbare cloth across her shoulders. She is fingering one torn corner. I want to ask her whether that is the cloth she brought from Africa, but the words remain locked behind my lips.

Her cloth reminds me of the dresses which Senhora Miranda sent with me as gifts for her. Josef and I take an elbow each and help her to her feet. We hold one of the dresses up against her. She looks ridiculous: a barefoot old slave woman wearing the cast-off satin dress of a rich society lady. We look at one another. We don't know what to say to her.

When she is alone with him, they speak their African language. If there are others present, they speak Portuguese. But when I am alone with her, she prefers to speak English.

We help her into her hut. There is a low bed, a table and a chair, a couple of bowls and buckets, and some clothing hanging from iron spikes driven into the mud walls. Josef rolls out a sleeping mat on the smooth mud floor.

"Your father, Tomba, made that bed for me," she tells me. "But since he ... since he left us, I have never slept on it. Now I need to take a nap. That storytelling has tired me out. Josef, come for me later, I beg you."

Josef takes me up to the casa grande where Senhor Fonseca, the manager, stays. A room has been prepared for me in the quarters at the back. It has a good bed and a table and a chair. There is a basin and a jug, and a bucket of warm water. I wash the mud off my feet. The first thing I'll do when Senhora Miranda gives me my freedom is to buy myself a pair of boots. That will mark me as a free man. And then, once I have saved a hundred milreis, I'll buy a young slave to keep them polished.

Josef takes me across to the kitchen and introduces me to his wife, Wono, and another woman called Ayo. They make a big fuss over me and pretend to be upset that I don't remember them. They claim they have known me since the day I was born. Stupid old women, talking such nonsense. What is that to me?

But they make me sit at the kitchen table and they give me a good meal. Senhora Fonseca comes in while I am eating. I make to stand up but she stops me and asks after the health of Senhora Miranda and Senhorita Elizabeth.

When I have eaten, Josef takes me to see the sugar mill. On the way, we meet some of the field slaves returning from their work. They file into the yard in the dark, dragging heavy legs, tripping over the ruts in the track, too weary even to talk. Josef introduces me to an old graybeard called Olukoya who is in charge of them. He is Ayo's husband. It seems I should remember him, too, but I don't. My childhood before Salvador is a blank. What is there about this place that's worth remembering, anyway?

One visit to the mill is enough for me. At the back of the kettle house, a roaring furnace sends great orange flames flickering upwards, silhouetting the glistening naked bodies of the stokers. This is surely the hell that old Father Isaac depicts in his homilies. I would not survive here for a day, let alone an eternity. I bless Senhora Miranda that she took me away from all this to the heavenly cleanliness and comfort of her home in Salvador.

When we enter the store where the sugar cones are seasoning, we meet Olukoya again. His gang of field hands is back at work. At this time of the year, during the safra, the sugar harvest, they labor eighteen hours a day.

Josef

Zacharias worships Senhora Miranda.

When the Senhora was just a country girl, growing up here, at the Engenho de Cima, Sister Ama worked in the casa grande. Senhorita Miranda had no sisters and there were no white girls of her age in the vicinity. The nearest engenho was a dead estate, a *fogo morto*, called the Engenho do Meio, where my friend Fifi was the caretaker, living a hand-to-mouth existence.

Miranda's younger brother, Alexandré, teased her without mercy. Her mother, the old Senhora, was a cold, unhappy woman. Sister Ama became Senhorita Miranda's elder sister. Hers was a shoulder to cry on.

When Senhor Gavin married Senhorita Miranda and took her away to Salvador, she was little more than a child. In the city, she had to grow up quickly. I saw all this because I was the messenger. Once a week I would sail the old Senhor's boat across All Saints Bay to the city and back. Depending on the wind, the trip each way might take a full day.

Senhora Miranda came back to the Engenho for the birth of her daughter, Senhorita Elizabeth; and Zacharias was born in the very same bed just a week later. That renewed the bond between the two mothers, though one was a slave and the other the daughter of the slave master.

No doubt Senhora Miranda thought she was doing Sister Ama a great service by taking Zacharias away to Salvador after the troubles. But I wonder. Senhora Miranda has become the boy's foster mother. And yet, how could that be, with him a black slave and she a rich white slave owner, indeed, now, his owner?

Zacharias

I brought thirty sheets of paper. I took them from Senhor Gavin's cabinet, just two or three sheets at a time. If I had taken more, Senhor Gavin might have noticed. I can hear him telling me that paper and ink don't grow on trees. I couldn't risk him accusing me of theft. Senhor Gavin trusts me.

This looks as if it's going to be a long story. I may run out of paper before the end. Josef says the only paper here is in the store and that is kept under lock and key. We discuss the problem with my mother and she says she will try to be brief.

Ama's story

That night, the Bedagbam raiders assembled at an abandoned homestead. They had captured about twenty men and one young boy called Suba. I was the only girl. Like me, Suba had been dragged from his mother's home. I did my best to comfort him and he responded by treating me as if I were his elder sister.

The attack came just before dawn. All the Bedagbam, including the guards, were asleep. Itsho and his party crept into the camp, naked and oiled. Silently they slashed four of the sleepers with sharp blades. Then quickly and just as silently, they slipped away. Their victims' screams woke their fellows to a scene of bloody terror and confusion. It was as if they had been attacked by ghosts. Their leader, Abdulai, the one who had raped me, was the first to come to his senses. He yelled to them to run for their horses, which were tethered nearby. As they emerged from the ruined buildings, carrying their saddles and their weapons, Itsho and his men fired their poisoned arrows. They targeted the horses, too, but Abdulai and some of his men managed to mount, and once they were on horseback, Itsho's men were little match for them. I couldn't see much of this but, from the noise, I could guess what was going on. At first, I was excited, confident of the outcome. Then, when it became clear that the attack had failed, I cried in despair.

After the Bedagbam had counted their dead, men and horses, Abdulai sent Suba and me to collect water from a stream, with Damba as our guard. On the way down, there was a dead body in our path. Damba turned it over with his boot. I kept telling myself, "Itsho escaped, Itsho escaped," over and over. We collected the water. On the way back the vultures were picking at the corpse. There was nothing we could do. Damba wouldn't let us stop to dig a grave.

Then we came across another body, naked except for a loincloth.

A horse's hoof had crushed Itsho's skull. I knew every muscle on that beautiful body of his.

Strangely enough, I was quite calm. I suppose I must have prepared myself for the shock. I set the calabash of water down and knelt beside him. I laid my cheek on his chest. His body was still warm. Damba was good. Using Suba as an interpreter, he asked me who it was. I told him it was my husband. Abdulai's orders were to bury only the Bedagbam dead, but we were out of sight of the camp. Suba helped me cover Itsho's body with branches to keep the vultures off. Then we went back to the camp to deliver the calabashes of water. Damba let me collect a hoe, my mother's hoe, one he had stolen from us. I dug a shallow grave while Damba and Suba went down to the stream. I washed Itsho's body. For the first time in my life, I spoke to the ancestors, asking them to forgive me, a mere woman, for addressing them directly. I begged them to accept Itsho's spirit. Then Suba and Damba helped me lift his body into the grave. We covered it with stones to protect it from the hyenas.

Zacharias

My tears fall on the paper, making the ink run. I have to ask her to stop.

"My Mother," I ask, "was Itsho my father?"

As soon as I say that, I know how stupid it is. Last night she mentioned another name, Tomba, I think. She said that my father was called Tomba and that he had made her bed for her.

"From his place with our ancestors," she says, "Itsho has watched over me all my life. I am sure he has watched over you and my granddaughter, Nandzi Ama, too. But your father was Tomba, my second and only other love."

She stretches out her hands. I give her mine and she squeezes them. Then she draws me to her and for the first time I embrace her. She is Ama. She is My Mother. We cry together. After a while, she wipes her dead eyes with her old cloth.

CHAPTER THREE

Ama

I do not understand Kwame.

First: his name. He prefers to use the Christian name Miranda chose for him, rather than the name his father and mother gave him.

Second: he says he doesn't remember Tomba or me. I am his mother. Tomba and I brought him up. He was a good boy. His early years were carefree. The old Senhora put me in charge of the kitchen stores, so he seldom went hungry. For his first six years, he ran naked with the other children. He was usually asleep when Tomba arrived at night, so it was only on Sundays and Saints' Days that he saw his father. The three of us would spend that day working in my allotment. Almost before the boy could walk, Tomba started to take him to the forest to hunt and trap and fish.

The Christmas after Kwame turned seven, the storeman issued him and his age-mates with their first cotton shifts. I remember my boy's pride when he wore clothes for the first time. The following year, he began to do odd jobs and run messages.

I began with the best of intentions: I would teach him to speak Asante and to read and write Portuguese as well as speaking it; but as time went by, my remaining eye began to lose its strength. I often felt tired. So I told him stories instead. Stories from Africa. Stories of my own happy childhood. But I never did tell him about Abdulai and what came after.

"Tell him," Olukoya urged me.

"Later," I insisted. "He is still too young to understand."

By the time he was old enough to understand, it was too late.

Of all this, he says he remembers nothing. It is as if Miranda has succeeded in wiping Tomba and me from his memory. Why would she do that? She has kept my son from me all these years, so long that I had given up hope of ever seeing him again. Then, suddenly, she decides to send him to the Engenho on a visit. Why?

I need to consult Olukoya and Ayo, and Josef and Wono.

Then there is the matter of the paper. If Miranda has been so good to Kwame, why could he not have simply passed on my request to her? He says he had to steal the paper from Senhor Gavin. I didn't bring him up to be a thief.

He tells me he has already filled four sheets, writing on both sides, and I have only just begun my tale. I may have to leave some parts out, but how can I decide in advance which to omit?

Ama's story

Abdulai and his Bedagbam brigands marched us across the plain to their capital, Yendi. There they kept us behind walls and put us to work. Our numbers grew day by day as they brought in more and more captives. Suba already knew some of their language, Dagbani, and he quickly became quite fluent. They started to use him as an interpreter, and that gave him a chance to learn some of their secrets. It was Suba who told me what lay behind our capture.

A few years before, the Bedagbam had fought a war with the Asante. The Asante were on foot and the Bedagbam were mounted, but the Asante had guns and the Bedagbam horses were hearing gunfire for the first time, so the Asante won the day. Now, at that time, I had never seen or heard a gun. We don't even have a word in our language for such a thing, so Suba had a job describing it to me, especially since his understanding was as small as mine.

The Asante made the Bedagbam pay for losing the war. Every year, at the Asante harvest festival, the Bedagbam had to deliver to them so many pieces of cotton cloth, so many pieces of silk cloth, herds of goats and flocks of sheep, and five hundred human beings, men, women, and children. The Asante agreed that the Bedagbam would not have to enslave their own kin, so their ruler, the Ya Na, sent out raiding parties like Abdulai's to steal whatever they could and to hunt our people.

The commander of the Asante forces had stayed behind in Yendi after the war. I learned later that he was called Nana Koranten Péte. One day he and the Ya Na came to inspect us. It was as if we were goats offered for sale in the market. The two of them took a fancy to me. I can't think why. Water was scarce and I was filthy from my work in their shea-butter factory. The Ya Na wanted to take me for his use but Koranten Péte said no, I was already the property of the Asante king.

The next day I witnessed an execution: the two guards who had slept while Itsho and his men slipped into their camp had their heads cut off. I saw it all again that night in my sleep and woke up with a scream in my throat.

I decided to escape. I stole a cutlass and a water bottle and hid them. I must have been mad to think I could succeed. Even if I had managed to elude their horsemen, I would have had to make a journey of several days across open country, without food or water, friends or landmarks along the way.

I remember the dogs howling after me in the dark as I ran through the empty streets of the town. The path I took into the bush soon petered out. I was already exhausted from my day's work, hungry and thirsty. Soon I was lost, swinging my cutlass without conviction in an attempt to cut a passage through the thorn bushes.

Then I recognized the rasping cough of a leopard. I climbed a tree and tied myself to the highest branch I could reach. Damba found me there the next day, fast asleep, with the marks of the leopard's paws imprinted on the sand below. He had to stand on his horse's saddle to lift me down.

The Ya Na sentenced me to death. I didn't mind; I had nothing to look forward to in my life. And yet, I cannot deny it, I was scared.

Fortunately, the night out had left me with a high fever. For some reason I did not understand, they decided to let me recover before killing me. I was put in Damba's care and his mother nursed me slowly back to health. In the end it was Koranten Péte who saved my life. He decided that he would give me as a gift to one of the Asante royals.

Zacharias

I read what I have written; I read it aloud to my mother. It is a strange experience. I speak in her voice and she listens. It is almost as if I become her and she becomes me. The first time, she lets me read the whole passage without interruption. When I come to the end, she lavishes praise on me. I explain that I have had plenty of practice; Senhor Gavin dictates his official letters to me. Sometimes I have to do a second draft. When he has signed the letter, I make a copy in our letter book.

My mother asks me to read the passage again, slowly.

From time to time she stops me and asks me to cross out a word and substitute another—small corrections only, or second thoughts. I am proud to be able to serve her in this way.

My mother is a courageous woman. You wouldn't think it to look at her now. I try to imagine her as a young woman. In Africa. A beautiful young woman in Africa.

Ama's story

Most of us had to walk, but I was lucky—Koranten Péte selected a few of us to travel with him by canoe down the river Daka. The new sights made me forget my terrible predicament. Enormous trees lined the banks, each one different, some a mass of flowers, white, yellow, red, even blue. We saw crocodiles and hippos and, late one afternoon, while Koranteng Péte was looking for a place to camp, our way was blocked by a family of elephants. A huge bull, with torn ears and one tusk shorter than the other, stood guard on a sand bank, head and trunk raised, challenging us, while his tribe cavorted in the water behind him. One of the Asante guards raised his flintlock rifle, but Koranteng Péte slapped it down with a stern reprimand.

Then there were the birds. The trees were full of so many different kinds of birds, birds I had never seen before, singing birdsongs I had never heard. The Asante man who sat behind me knew the name of every one and had a story to tell about each of them. They called him Akwasi Anoma, the bird man. My problem with him was that he couldn't keep his hands off me.

After some days, we arrived at a large town called Kafaba. It was situated on high ground overlooking a wide river called the Volta. After the morning mist cleared, one could see land on the other side, but it was far away. Koranteng Péte left us there to wait for those who were coming overland. He put Akwasi Anoma in charge. He was a brutal man and I suffered badly from his attentions. I thought again of escape but deep down I knew that it was only a dream. My home was far away. I had no idea how to find it and the countryside was full of danger. So I turned my thoughts to Kafaba town and the people who lived there.

Akwasi Anoma decided to find a room to rent. He made me follow him, carrying his bundle on my head. The first thing I saw as I trudged up the hill was an area fenced with cut bamboo. Horses and asses, oxen, cows, and goats roamed freely within it, searching the parched ground for a blade of grass; but there were humans there, too: slaves, hundreds of them, many of them all but naked, using scraps of cloth or bundles of leaves to hide their shame and to shelter from the burning sun. Their ribs stuck out and their skin was wrinkled. They were chained to one another in fives and sixes. The end of each chain was attached to a stake driven into the ground. There was nowhere they could go to empty their bowels, so they had to do their business where they sat, exposed to the gaze of their fellows and passersby. One woman, who had a baby on her lap, a poor creature of skin and bones, put her hands under her breasts and lifted them to show me that they were quite empty. Then she held out those same hands and moved them to her lips, begging for food; but I had nothing to offer. All I could do was shrug and show her my own open palms. After all these years I still have her picture embedded in my mind. I remember wondering then, as I looked into her eyes, whether I was seeing my own future.

Zacharias

I ask my mother about the vision which she saw in the eyes of that slave woman in Africa. Can anyone see into the future? She says the child in that woman's lap had little time to live, and the woman, too, perhaps. They had no future.

"I am lucky," she says. "My own child survived into manhood and now he has a child of his own."

She is talking about me.

She asks me how many sheets of paper I have left.

Ama's story

They ferried us across the river, ten at a time, first the women, then the men. It took a whole day. Early the next morning, Koranten Péte poured libation and addressed his ancestors. Soon we set off on a long march through the bush, led by drummers and musketeers. Koranten Péte sat in a hammock, carried by four of our men. The rest followed in twelves, manacled wrist to wrist in pairs and spaced a stride apart along a heavy chain. Each of the men carried a head load. So did we women, but we were not chained.

The drummers set a steady pace and we soon got into our stride. Then something strange happened to me. I was possessed. I found myself first humming and then singing a dirge, one I had heard at funerals but never sung; but now the words were different. I felt Itsho's presence and he seemed to be dictating to me as I am now dictating this story to you, my son. I felt that my spirit had left my body and that I was floating at a great height, looking down on our caravan. I sang to the rhythm of the drums:

"Oh, you our ancestors, our grandparents

"And their parents; and their parents and grandparents."

And then the chorus:

"Hear our voice,

"Hear our lamentation."

And then I addressed them again:

"Oh, you our ancestors, all those who in the dim mists of the past

"Have lived upon this earth and have gone before us into the world of the spirits:

"Advise us, help us,

"Succor us."

And after each short verse, the chorus again.

"We, too, have died and yet we live still.

"We are as walking corpses.

"We have no drink to offer

"But we beg and beseech you:

"Hear our voice,

"Hear our lamentation.

"Our freedom has been taken from us

"Our spirits are chained to our dead bodies.

"Who will perform the rites which will free our spirits

"And send them to your world?

"Hear us, advise us, fortify us,

"Give us back life; give us back hope.

"Hear our voice,

"Hear our lamentation."

And as I sang, the other women began to hum, and then, as they picked up the words, they joined in the chorus; first those near me and then those ahead and those behind. And when I came to the end, one of them shouted, "Again," and we sang it again and again until everyone knew the words.

Though the singing of dirges is women's work, even the men joined in. Koranten Péte could have given instructions to the guards to force silence upon us, or he could have ordered the drummers to rest their sticks, but he didn't. In Africa, only a madman or a fool interrupts a conversation with the ancestors.

Then we came to a river. The drummers stopped drumming and the musketeers fired volleys into the air to frighten off the crocodiles. We waded across. The rhythm had been broken. We didn't sing again.

Zacharias

That is a pagan song. She should have sung a prayer to God, or Jesus, or Mary. I suppose I cannot blame her, since she was as ignorant of religion as she was of guns. As Father Isaac says, God has given the Portuguese the task of bringing the blacks from the pagan darkness of Africa into the Christian light. In Africa, all they have to look forward to is the certainty of eternal hellfire. In Brazil, they have the chance of salvation.

I ask her, "My Mother, have you been saved?"

"Saved? From slavery? By whom?" she asks. "It is too late for that. Kwame, my time is short. Let us continue."

Ama's story

You wouldn't think it to look at me now, but in those days I must have been quite a pretty girl. The guards were forever flirting with me. One in particular—a tease called Mensa—made a point of walking alongside me. I asked him to teach me their language. That amused him. Mensa told me all sorts of stories. Most of them seemed to me far-fetched, but they passed the time. He told me that the Asante king, the

Asantehene, had three thousand, three hundred and thirty-three wives. (To do that, he first had to teach me how to count in his language: baako, mienu, miensa is how they say one, two, three.) He said that the King's wives were the finest, the most beautiful women in Asante. And he said that all the finest, most beautiful women in Asante were married to the King.

"If the King sees a beautiful woman," he said, "he will take her, even if she is another man's wife, or if she is a slave. If the King sees you, he might marry you; but, be warned: if you then take a lover and get found out, you must expect to be tortured and to die."

There was no way that I could know then that I would indeed meet the Asante king one day. But that comes later in my story.

After a few days, we entered a dark forest of gigantic trees. It was only along our road that the sunlight reached the ground. Great multicolored butterflies flitted across that sunlit stretch, but on either side there was gloom. Tiny shrill-voiced birds with bright red and yellow and blue breasts and long curved beaks swept out of the darkness to suck the nectar from the wild flowers that grew in the tangled roadside jungle. The scent of rotting vegetation filled the air. We had never experienced anything like that before. We were creatures of the savannah and unused to the humidity. Our bodies and clothing were drenched in sweat.

The forest pressed in on us. From its depths came strange, discordant sounds, a chorus of screeching, howling, and wailing. Mensa said they were the voices of spirits, angry at our invasion of their private domain.

Zacharias

It is Sunday. My mother says it is a day of rest. I tell her I would like to go to Mass. By this time Iphigenia will be sitting with Carlota outside our church in Salvador. We slaves are allowed to attend this church but we have to stand at the back. They don't allow small children because they sometimes cry and disturb the whites. Iphigenia usually sits outside in the shade of a tree with the other mothers while I go inside.

My mother says there will be no Mass here today. The priest only visits the Engenho two or three times a year.

It turns out that the only ones who will get some real rest today are my quill and ink and paper. We are at my mother's allotment and there is work to be done.

In spite of her stiff joints, my mother gets down on her hands and knees and moves along the rows, gently feeling the heads of the carrots, loosening the soil around them with her fingers and pulling up the weeds. I am surprised at her energy but concerned that the work is too much for her.

"My Mother, let me do it," I insist.

"You are a town boy," she says. "Life in Miranda's big house in Salvador has made you soft."

"Not so," I reply. "Behind our quarters, Senhora Miranda has a vegetable garden and she has made me her head gardener. She says she is a farm girl at heart, and sometimes she is homesick when she thinks of the Engenho."

"The hypocrite," my mother says. "When she was growing up here, she hardly ever set foot outside the casa grande. She showed no interest at all in the workings of her father's engenho, let alone our allotments."

She sits back on her haunches.

"When I still had some sight," she says, "I used to weed with a hoe. Now I have to use my fingers to distinguish the useful plants from weeds."

In spite of her protestations, she soon tires. I help her to her seat on a rock and she lets me do the work. Today we talk about gardening, about compost and insect pests. At last we have found an interest that we share. While I work, she asks me questions about my life in Salvador, about Senhor Gavin and Senhora Miranda, about Iphigenia and Carlota and Iphigenia's parents, about how it is to be a slave in town, about the books which Senhor Gavin has given me to read. She asks searching questions, some of which I find it difficult to answer. To look at this old woman with her shrunken body, the grey stubble on her shaven skull, and her staring, sightless eyes, you would hardly guess the depth of her wisdom and experience.

Chapter Four

Ama's story

If you had brought more paper, I would have told you stories of the time I spent living in the palace of Nana Osei Kwadwo, the fourth king of Asante. I would have told you of the gold ornaments he wore on state occasions, of his golden crown, of his gold breast-plate, of his necklaces, bracelets, anklets, finger rings, all solid gold and of such a weight that he could not walk without assistance; I would have told you of the ivory horns and *fontomfrom* drums and those who played them, celebrating Nana's great valor, and of the enormous multicolored umbrella which shaded him from the sun; I would have told you of his three thousand, three hundred and thirty-three wives whose faces only eunuchs were permitted to see; and of how one day he chucked me under the chin, looked me in the eye, asked my name, and said I was a pretty girl and that if he had been a few years younger, he might have married me. I would have told you of the orgy of bloodletting which followed his death. A person of the Asantehene's status must not arrive unaccompanied at the village of his ancestors. Slaves and subjects must be killed to join his retinue of spirits. Osei Kwadwo's cohort included all his favorite wives. It was my singular good fortune that, by the time he discovered my existence, he had already outlived his desire.

If you had brought more paper, I would have told you also of the Golden Stool, which the priest Okomfo Anokye conjured out of the heavens as a home for the soul of the Asante nation, and how that soul passes from the care of one Asantehene to that of his successor.

And, talking of successors, I might (only might) have told you of Osei Kwame, who succeeded Osei Kwadwo as the custodian of the Golden Stool—Osei Kwame, who came to power when he was still a lad, as a consequence of an assassination carried out in public, before my very eyes (which could then see as well as yours can now) by a giant Chief Executioner called Konkonti.

But these rich and powerful kings have their own historians whose fulltime work it is to remember and proclaim in fitting perorations their great victories; and to drown their defeats in the swamp of lost memories. The poor and humble, slaves like me and pawns like my friend Esi, have no historians and, like the kings' defeats, our lives are quickly forgotten. So I will use our small stock of paper to tell you our stories, rather than theirs.

Soon after we arrived in Kumase, the Asante capital, Koranten Péte, whom you have already met, gave me as a gift to the Queen Mother, Asantehemaa Konadu Yaadom. It was Konadu Yaadom who found my name Nandzi difficult to pronounce and named me, instead, Ama, in the casual way the Portuguese name their dogs; and it was in Konadu Yaadom's household that I got to know her son, who was destined first to succeed Osei Kwadwo as Asantehene and then to select me, almost by chance, as his first lover; and, if he had had his way, his first wife.

When Konadu Yaadom and Koranten Péte got to know of the young king's infatuation with me, they decided that I was a danger to the Asante state, I a humble slave girl of obscure origin, at least to them. Someone hid a bag of gold dust in my rolled-up sleeping mat. Then Konadu Yaadom arranged for it to be found, identified it as her property, and accused me of theft. I was taken to the Asantehene's court, found guilty, and sentenced to be banished and sold to the white men at the coast.

My friend Esi happened to be in the court, minding Konadu Yaadom's infant child. She was outraged at the injustice of it all and spoke up bravely on my behalf. For her impudence they sentenced her at once to join me, my loving, lovely, stupid, brave friend, Esi. All that remains for me now, before we leave Kumase, is to introduce her to you.

Esi's father was a Fante, like Josef, from the coast. Esi taught me everything: the Asante language, their music, how to dance Adowa, and all the tricks that one needed to survive in the household of Konadu Yaadom. And the gossip! Nothing happened in that city that didn't reach the ears of my friend Esi.

One day we were sitting alone together and gossiping. Our conversation turned to the Asantehene, and I told her that I was sure that he was ill and didn't have long to live. Her jaw dropped and she stared at me with an expression of fear that I had never seen in her face before. Then she rose to her feet and started to sing a Fante dirge and dance the Chief Executioner's dance. By the time I managed to calm her down, the sweat was running down her face and arms. What she told me then made me sweat, too. Immediately after Osei Kwadwo's death, many would be killed to join him on his journey and we, his slaves, would be in the greatest danger.

It was Esi who saved me from a sudden death.

A steep, outside wooden staircase led up to Konadu Yaadom's first-floor bedroom. A small room under the staircase was used as a store, a sort of dump for broken pots, cracked wooden pestles, and mortars which had become too short to use.

Esi was a great flirt. Making sure that Konadu Yaadom would be away for some time, she persuaded one of the palace carpenters to fix the hinges on the door and install a new iron lock. When the King died, we hid in that tiny room for three days. It was only when we were sure that the slaughter of the innocents had come to an end that Esi decided that it was safe for us to emerge from our hiding place.

It was Esi's foresight that saved us from accompanying Osei Kwadwo on his journey to the ancestors.

Her courage and foolhardy intolerance of injustice now led to her joining me on my journey to meet the white man at Elmina on the coast.

Zacharias

My mother is a great story teller. But I wonder: does she really expect me to swallow all this stuff? Does this Africa really exist other than in her imagination? I may be her son, but I am no longer a child.

"My Mother," I ask, "are these stories you are telling me really true?"

She is offended.

"My son Kwame, do you think I am telling you lies?"

I try to explain. Her stories are so fantastic, I find it hard to believe them. She calms down.

"Wait," she says. "You've heard nothing yet."

Ama's story

It was twenty days since our coffle of slaves had left Kumase.

As we topped the crest of a hill, Esi cried, "Ama, look!"

In the middle distance, row upon row of coconut palms; beyond the palms, a strip of white sand; beyond the beach, the great white-flecked expanse of the ocean. The breakers rolled in upon the shore with a distant roar.

Esi clutched my arm and pointed at the seemingly countless canoes, some of them scudding across the surface with the wind in their sails, each with its crew of tiny figures.

"Is that the sea?" I asked our guard Mensa.

Even on the open savannah in the dry season, you can't see so far into the distance. Out there, beyond the rows of coconut palms, there were no hills and trees to block the view. I had imagined that the great water would be like the Volta River, only wider. I was so ignorant; it shames me to think of it. Mensa laughed, amused at my astonishment. He told me that the water was salty, that if you drink it, it will make you vomit. I thought he was teasing me.

"Why would anyone want to put salt in it?" I asked him. "And where would they get so much salt? There must be a lot of water there. Next you will be telling me that it is blue because someone has poured accassie dye into it."

The waves broke up in white foam as they approached the shore.

"See how it boils," said Mensa. "You can cook green plantain inside."

When we got down onto the beach, I saw small boys playing in the surf. The sand burned the soles of my feet. I dipped them in the water.

"I will make you eat the green plantain I cook inside," I told Mensa.

Zacharias

When she told me that she didn't believe the guard when he said the sea was salty, I laughed. Then she asked me whether I could explain to her why it is salty and why it looks blue. I felt stupid because I had no answer. I shall have to ask Senhor Gavin.

Ama's story

At the end of the curve of the bay, there rose a great block, sparkling white in the sunlight.

Mensa laughed and pointed.

"That is the house of the white man, the Dutch governor. Did I not tell you that the whites are twice as tall as normal human beings? It is because they are so tall that they need such big houses. That one is called Elmina Castle."

I gave up, not knowing what to believe.

Two men came out of the building. One was black. Though the skin of the other was lighter in color, tawny, he was of normal size. Like his fellow, he wore a peculiar red garment, somewhat the worse for wear; but apart from that, he looked just like a pale version of a normal man. I thought to ask Mensa if this was a white man, but Mensa was nowhere to be seen. I never did see him again.

These two also seemed to be guards, judging from their long whips.

I was at the head of the line of women with Esi beside me.

"This way," called the brown one in a sort of broken Asante. He was looking in my direction, but I thought that he was speaking to someone behind me.

I looked back and saw the shackles being removed from the first of our men. Then the guard grabbed my arm roughly and manhandled me across two short wooden bridges. Esi tried to follow me, but the other guard restrained her. We called out to each other.

The guard dragged me through a dark passage, into a great courtyard, and down another dark passage. Then he used a key to open an iron door, pushed me through the opening, and banged the door shut.

I gripped the iron bars and looked out into the courtyard. The stone floor was drenched in sunlight. Then I heard a sound behind me. Startled, I turned. In the darkness all I could see was the whites of many pairs of eyes. I pressed my back against the gate. A child was sobbing. Now I could see women sitting shoulder to shoulder with their backs to the walls of the room. Others sat and lay on the damp stone floor. I took a step forward, started to take a deep breath, and then as quickly pinched my nostrils. The air was thick with the foul smell of unwashed bodies and old shit and piss. Apart from the gate where I stood, there were no other openings for light or air.

CHAPTER FIVE

Ama's story

When I woke, there was not a single glimmer of light in the dungeon.

The smell struck me and I wanted to vomit. The air was unpleasantly hot and humid, yet the floor I lay on was cold and damp. I was thirsty and I wanted to piss. I screwed up my eyes but I could see nothing. I could hear the sleep sounds of many women and children.

I tried to think. That very morning I had been walking along the beach, watching the naked boys playing in the waves, breathing deeply in air which had the fresh smell of the sea. Now I was in a place worse than death. Or is this death? I wondered. The dungeon had already been crowded when we arrived. All the other women in the caravan had followed us, one by one. The women who had already been there some time—how long? I wondered—abused us in several languages: my own, Asante, and others I did not understand.

We were all victims of the same unseen oppressor and yet we quarreled amongst ourselves. (If it weren't for Olukoya's leadership, we might be doing that here, too.)

I heard a sound from the courtyard. A key turned in the lock. Esi was sleeping next to me, nearer to the gate. I shook her gently and whispered her name in her ear.

The gate opened. Esi sat up.

"What is it?" she asked. "Where am I?"

A man entered, carrying an oil lamp, keeping it low, looking at the sleeping faces. His own face remained in the shadows. He brought the lamp up close to Esi's face. Then he said something, just one or two words, in a strange language. He grabbed Esi's arm and pulled her upright. She gasped and stretched for me, but it was too late. The man dragged her through the gate and banged it shut. A woman groaned in her sleep.

"Ama," Esi cried but her voice was muffled as if a hand had been placed over her mouth.

Silence settled over the dungeon. I lay awake, not knowing what to do, what to think.

Time passed. Then there was the sound of the key turning in the lock again. The gate opened and Esi was pushed inside. She was sobbing deliriously. I stepped over bodies in the dark, guiding her to her place. I tried to comfort her.

"What happened?" I asked, but Esi could not speak.

I dozed. The screeching of metal on metal woke me as the dungeon gate swung open again. A guard entered, shouting at us, kicking, cracking his whip in the dark, forcing us onto our feet and out.

I blinked and rubbed my eyes. (I had two eyes then. It is only now that I have lost the sight of both, that I have learned to value them.) It was afternoon. The sun lit up one wall and half of the stone floor of the courtyard. Two more guards lounged against the wall in a corner, flicking their whips at one another. They were barefooted and stripped to the waist.

One shouted at us. The other laughed. More women came streaming out past the iron gate. The second guard clapped his hands, lining us up against the walls. We stood there, confused and uncertain, flexing our limbs and looking around. Esi stretched her arms and yawned. Some of the women began to chatter. One began to sing a dirge in a high-pitched voice. The first guard silenced us with a harsh command and a crack of his whip.

I stood in the shade and hugged myself. What now? I wondered.

I looked around the courtyard. The stone flags were smooth. Many feet must have walked on them before mine. I raised my eyes and examined the walls. The sunlight reflected off the whitewashed surface made me blink again. I looked away to avoid the glare. High above me, I caught a glimpse of a head of golden hair.

The first guard prodded the women at the end of the row with the butt of his whip, urging them to stand upright and look ahead. They murmured, sullen, confused, but somehow resisting him. The guard craned his neck, looking up at that head of golden hair.

I was fifth from the end. By my side stood Esi, short, plump Esi, her eyes meekly on her feet. I looked up and, with a start, again caught sight of what I had only glimpsed before. The golden-haired, red-faced god in his spotless white uniform astonished me. That must be a real white man, I thought. I nudged Esi and, with a nod of my head, directed her gaze up at him. Esi stared, her mouth open.

"That is the pig," she muttered to me. "I am sure. That is the pig."

It was the man who had had her the night before, in the dark courtyard, against the wall, without ceremony. That morning she had told me of the pain in her loins and the humiliation and degradation of being used like that.

I stared at him, wondering what was going on, trying to make sense of the golden pig-god, the rapist, the first real white man I had seen.

I saw him raise the five fingers of his right hand and then move the index finger from left to right. The guard who had driven us out of the dungeon placed a hand on my shoulder. I flinched, but he held me firmly. The guard looked up at the pig-god. I saw him nod and guessed what lay in store for me.

“Mama, the pig wants to rape me,” I shrieked.

“The pig wants to rape her,” echoed one of the women, following my line of sight.

A third woman took up the call and then another, in language after language. In their voices I heard fear, anger, sympathy for me, and relief, selfish relief.

The guards screamed and cracked their whips, drowning the protests. One walked across to a corner of the courtyard and returned with a wooden chair, which he placed in the sunlight in view of the watcher above. Then he dragged me to it and barked an order. I didn’t understand.

“What do they want of me?” I wondered. “Perhaps the pig-god up there is a cannibal.”

I stood my ground, staring at the guard, hating him. He was a big man with broad shoulders and huge biceps. In Kumase, I thought, he would have been a professional executioner. Suddenly he grabbed me from behind, wrapping his arms around my waist. I screamed, but before I knew what had happened, I was standing on the chair. He reached up and grabbed my cloth and pulled it down. Next he ripped off my waist beads. The other two guards applauded. The women screamed at them.

I was now stark naked. I noticed the pig-god looking down at me and covered myself with my hands. For a moment, the other women were silent. Then they took up their wailing again. The guards started to herd them back into the dungeon. I heard Esi scream my name.

The big guard behind me grabbed hold of my wrists and pinned my arms behind my back. I cried out in pain but he held me immobile and exposed. The light-skinned guard looked up and the pig-god nodded. He forced my legs apart and stuck his index finger into me. I struggled to free myself from the grip of the guard behind me and screamed abuse at the light-skinned one. He withdrew his finger and raised it to the light to examine it. Then he put it under his nostrils and sniffed; after which he stood aside and raised the finger to show the pig-god, slowly nodding his head up and down.

The big guard released his grip. I stood silent and alone on the chair, crushed and humiliated. He returned my cloth and told me to get down. I covered myself and tried to recover a little of my dignity. Their whips cracking, the guards herded the last of the women back into the dungeon.

They gave me a bowl of rice and palm soup. It was the first real meal I had had since my arrival. I was hungry and ate quickly. As soon as I had finished, the big guard told me to get up.

"Where are you sending me?" I asked him.

"Oh, so you hear Fante?" he asked.

"Where are you sending me?" I repeated.

I have never hated any human being as I hated him at that moment.

"Never you mind," he said, taking my hand.

I resisted but he was far too strong for me.

He spoke to me again but I did not understand. In my fear, I remained silent. He directed me to a long, steep flight of black and white stone stairs, keeping close behind me. There was a landing, and then we turned to climb the second flight, this time of wood. The stairs creaked as we climbed, reminding me of Konadu Yaadom's staircase in Kumase. How happy I had been there. We had reached the level of the balcony from which I had seen the pig-god looking down into the courtyard, but he was nowhere to be seen. We turned a corner. Ahead of us there was a solid white door. Another guard was there, squatting on his haunches with his back against the wall. He signed to my guard to knock on the door.

There was a reply, just two words, but they meant nothing to me. My guard opened the door, pushed me into the room, and left me standing there. I heard the door close.

Zacharias

My mother tires easily. After that session she has to take a rest. I am not surprised. That was a difficult story for her to tell, even after all these years. Just listening to it and writing it down has left me drained.

She asks me, "Do you understand why I can never be a Christian?"

Out of respect for her suffering, I do not answer. When I get to know her better, I might talk to her about the power of forgiveness.

Ama's story

The man behind that door was Pieter de Bruyn, the Dutch governor. I would like to tell you about my life with him but if I do, we shall use up all the paper long before we reach the end of my story. In short, he was a lonely old man, getting to the end of his working life, and he fell in love with me. What could I do? It was not as if I had a choice. He treated me well and in the course of time, I became quite fond of him. He taught me to play chess. To start with, that was the only language we had in common, but he made the castle priest, a fat, lecherous fellow called van Schalkwyk, teach me English. He chose English rather than Dutch because he loved to read novels, and all the best novels are in English. His eyesight was failing and he thought I might help preserve it by reading to him.

Van Schalkwyk had ambitions to turn me into a Christian. I resisted, but I did learn to read the Bible. Even today, in my blindness, I pass the time by telling myself stories which I first read in that book.

Sometimes I called de Bruyn by his first name, especially when we were alone together; but as a rule, and always when there were others present, I called him Mijn Heer, that is, Sir, or My Master.

Mijn Heer's quarters were my world. Even if he had let me wander, where would I have gone? On a visit to the poor creatures imprisoned in the female dungeon? Or on an inspection of the male slaves; or the condemned cell where they kept men they would kill sometime later, when they had filled in the necessary forms?

Apart from Mijn Heer and the priest, I had only one other regular contact with the world outside my comfortable prison. That was a rich Fante lady by name Augusta, or, at any rate, that was the name which Mijn Heer had given her when, as a young girl, she had been married to him. I know what you are thinking: this Pieter de Bruyn had a special taste for young black female slaves. Well, to do him justice, that was not entirely true. Augusta had never been enslaved. Indeed, she had made a great deal of money from slave trading. And Mijn Heer had once had a white wife, a Dutch woman called Elizabeth, like your god-sister in Salvador. Mijn Heer took delight in dressing me up in all the fine European-style dresses Madam Elizabeth had kept in her trunk.

But I must be confusing you with all these characters who don't have much to do with my story. In some ways my life has been confusing. The Asante have a proverb which says it all: Obra kwan ye nkyinkyimiie, that is, the path of life is full of twists and turns. I well remember one of those twists and turns. (Are you writing all this down? You are wasting the paper.) Well, I had been living in comfort, eating well, wearing Madam Elizabeth's fine clothes, admiring my image in Mijn Heer's full-length mirror, lounging in his comfortable armchairs, reading my way through his library of English novels. One of them, by the way, was called Pamela, by Samuel Richardson. Have you read it? Mijn Heer gave me her name—he always called me Pamela. These Europeans cannot handle our African names. Or is giving your slave a name of your own choice just one more way to demonstrate your power? But I'm wandering. I want you to write this down.

One morning I was all alone in Mijn Heer's room. I took his telescope and sat myself on the broad sill at the west window. I aimed the instrument at a canoe that was being hollowed out on the far bank of the river and focused the lens. Progress was slow; the carvers had made several fires again, gradually burning away the heartwood of the log. Then I heard a noise, a great hubbub, shouting and laughter, the firing of muskets. Climbing down from my perch, I stretched out of the window and looked down.

Approaching the castle from the north was a long procession, a coffle of slaves. In the lead were musicians, beating drums to give a slow rhythm to the march, blowing horns, singing, and chanting. They were followed by merchants, responding to the greetings of the townspeople who lined their route in a condescending manner, heads held high, waving white handkerchiefs as if they were royal chiefs. Then the male slaves, who wore only loincloths. Through the telescope, I could see the dust-streaked sweat on their naked torsos. They walked in pairs, shackled, chained, and heavily loaded, taking one deliberate, painful step at a time, driven by the beat of thprieste drummers and the occasional flick of a whip. The female slaves followed, then the children, boys and girls, stolen from their parents or forfeited by them.

I closed my eyes. I went to the basin, washed my face and arms with cold water, and rubbed myself with a towel. Then I went back to the window and aimed the telescope, capturing each slave in turn in its round frame. Their necks were not bent, but it was only the need to support their head loads which kept them erect. I searched each face for some sign of dignity and courage, for some pride which had survived the suffering; but all I saw was sullen fear, despair, and an infinite weariness; or, worse, a blank, without expression, as if drained of all humanity. Face after face was the same.

Only once, in response to a whiplash on a naked back, did I see a man turn his head toward the oppressor with hatred in his eyes. I tried not to think. I shivered as if I had fever. I thought I might recognize a face, a face from Kumase or from home. I started to look at the female slaves. Their expressions were no different from the men's.

The priest van Schalkwyk had painted for me a vivid picture of hell, the destination of all unreformed sinners when they died, he said. These slaves were clearly all in some sort of hell already; and yet they were still alive. The living dead, I thought.

I went to the tall mirror, wiped the tears from my eyes,

and looked at my image. I kicked the sandals from my feet. I pulled the *doek* from my head and threw it to the floor. Staring at my own eyes, I removed my body cloth, folded it in two, and wrapped it around my waist. Then I examined the image of my body, the round limbs, the full breasts, the healthy skin.

I went back to the window. The procession had reached the parade ground, but instead of swinging left to enter the castle, it bore right and headed toward the market square in the town. As they turned, I caught a last glimpse of each face.

I knew now what I had been searching for: it was my own face, mine and Esi's. We had come to Elmina in just such a procession as this and I had forgotten; I had buried the unpleasant memories. And yet I was a stranger to nothing I saw down there. What have they done that their lives should have been taken from them like this? I wondered. What crime, what violation of an obscure taboo, what confrontation with some person of power, could merit such humiliation? I knew then that the gods of all slave traders are without mercy, without compassion.

Then I wondered, why am I here, up here, and they down there? Mijn Heer was guilty, I thought, and Augusta, too. Konadu Yaadom was guilty and Koranten Péte and all their people. Abdulai was guilty. And I was guilty, too, because I had been living a life of quiet comfort, preoccupied with my English lessons and my reading, while my sisters and brothers languished in the dungeons beneath my feet. Perhaps I was most guilty of all. Then the thought came to me: but what can I do? I had been reading the Book of Exodus. I thought of the child in the bulrushes. If I should become pregnant and bear Mijn Heer's son, I thought, I would call him Moses and, when he came to manhood, I would charge him with confronting the power of the slave traders.

I got down from the window sill, sank onto my haunches and, holding my head in my hands, dropped my forehead onto the wooden floor. Closing my eyes, I summoned Itsho.

"Itsho. Come to me. Tell me what I should do, what I can do, to stop this evil. Itsho, come."

I remained there without moving for several minutes. When I rose, I was more at peace, though the issue of what to do remained unresolved. I took the telescope again and went to the window. The procession had wound its way into the market square. Elephant teeth were being lifted from the heads of the fettered slaves, who then sank to the ground where they stood, rubbing their limbs. Young women of the town circulated amongst them, giving them water from their calabashes. The King emerged from his palace to survey the scene, surrounded by his elders and Augusta and the other noble ladies of the state.

I read nothing that day. I paced up and down the room. Real life had rudely burst in on the fantasy world in which I had been living. That night, I turned away from Mijn

Heer's advances.

"Is something wrong?" he asked.

"It is nothing," I replied, turning over on my side, hugging myself and pressing my face into the soft pillow.

Chapter Six

Ama's story

While I lived with Mijn Heer, he had several visitors whom I need to mention.

The first was an Irishman called Richard Brew. He ran a private slave-trading business at Anomabu, alongside the castle where the English company conducted its trade. Mijn Heer disliked the man but felt that he could not refuse hospitality to a fellow white. When Brew learned that I had lived in the Asantehene's palace, he immediately started to make plans to buy me from Mijn Heer and send me to Kumase with a young man who would use me as his interpreter to persuade the Asantehene to grant Brew a monopoly in the Asante slave trade. You will recognize that young man's name: Gavin Williams.

I wish my sight could be restored for just one moment, to witness your surprise. But yes, it is true. I first heard your Senhor Gavin's name many years ago in Africa. Nothing came of Brew's scheme.

The second visitor was David Williams, the captain of an English ship, *The Love of Liberty*. He was the uncle of Gavin Williams and had apprenticed his nephew to Brew. He was an old friend of Mijn Heer and he brought him the latest English novels. At the time of his visit, there had been war in the interior and, as a result, the dungeons of Elmina Castle were full. Mijn Heer did his best to persuade Williams to fill his ship with what they called Mina slaves. Williams was tempted by the low price, but he was scared that buying all his slaves from one place would increase the chance of rebellion. The two of them discussed these matters openly in my presence, as if I didn't exist or was too stupid to understand.

I think it was during Williams's visit that I first met Esi's pig-god face to face. He turned out to be Mijn Heer's right-hand man. His name was Jensen. He and the priest Hendrik van Schalkwyk hated each other. Jensen mocked the priest and refused to attend his church services; van Schalkwyk reported Jensen's activities with the female slaves to his masters in Holland. Their rules said that the employees of the Dutch company should not take advantage of the female slaves. Strictly speaking, Mijn Heer was also guilty, but van Schalkwyk was his friend and never reported him. When Jensen was in danger of dismissal, Mijn Heer offered him a way out—get married. Jensen selected a light-skinned (and light-headed) girl called Rose, who hailed from Cape Coast, just a few hours' walk from Elmina.

It was at their wedding that I met the last character I want to introduce to you.

Saying that reminds me that I have attended just three weddings in my life. That was the first, Miranda's was the second, and mine, to your father Tomba, a much more modest affair, was the last. When I have finished telling you this part of my story, I want to hear about your own wedding and about your wife and my granddaughter, Nandzi Ama. And you must promise to bring them with you on your next visit.

But I digress. The man I spoke of was one of three Cape Coast boys the English had sent to London to be trained as missionaries. One had taken ill and died and the second had gone mad; but the third, who left Africa as Kweku, returned as the Reverend Philip Quaque (still pronounced Kweku), chaplain of the European slave traders at the castle and missionary to the natives. His white English wife had brought with her to Cape Coast a library of children's books, intending to start a school but, like Mijn Heer's wife Elizabeth, she died not long after her arrival. It was her books, so I learned later, that van Schalkwyk had bought from the Reverend Philip Quaque to use in teaching me English. Van Schalkwyk invited Quaque to the wedding of Jensen and Rose. In the church, Mijn Heer introduced me to him and left me in his company. We had a brief, awkward conversation in English.

Soon after the wedding, Mijn Heer decided to inspect the most westerly Dutch outpost at a place called Axim, traveling in a small ship. This was the first time I was to be left on my own. I was apprehensive and tried to persuade him not to go, or at least to postpone his trip. He comforted me with a promise that when he returned he would get van Schalkwyk to marry us. I counted the days.

At long last, the small ship returned. I rushed down to the quay but there was no sign of Mijn Heer on deck. I found him lying on his bunk, bathed in sweat, his bedclothes soaked. When he opened his eyes, I saw that they were yellow. The crew manhandled him through the door and laid him on a rough litter. At my wits' end, I sent for Augusta. Together we nursed him, day and night, but his condition grew steadily worse. The disease which struck him down is called the yellow jack.

Knowing he had not long to live, he sent for van Schalkwyk and, in my presence, dictated his last will and testament. In it he granted me my freedom. He left me also all late Elizabeth's clothing, all his English books, all his furniture and china and silverware, his gold ring, and five ounces of gold dust. He had just enough strength to sign the document. That night, five days after his return from Axim, he died.

As we walked back from the Dutch cemetery, Augusta asked me, "Sister Ama, what will you do now?" I was too tired to think. During that last week, I had hardly slept.

When I reached the top floor, I was surprised to see that the door of Mijn Heer's room was open. Jensen and Rose were there.

"What do you want?" Jensen snapped at me.

"Please, sir," I told him, "I am very tired. I had little sleep while I was nursing Mijn Heer. I thought ..."

He interrupted me. "Never mind what you thought. I am the 'Mijn Heer' now. You will sleep tonight where you came from and where you belong."

At that moment, van Schalkwyk knocked and entered.

"Ah, Jensen," he said, "I have been searching all over for you. They told me I would find you here."

"Mijn Heer Jensen, if you please," the pig-god told him. "I act as Director-General until the Company Directors rule otherwise. What do you want?"

Van Schalkwyk replied meekly. "Mijn Heer Jensen," he said, "Mijn Heer made a will before he died. I have it here."

He drew the document from his waistcoat.

"He appointed me his sole executor. I wondered if we might fix a time for it to be read to the officers."

"Let me see that," Jensen demanded. He took the sheet of paper to Mijn Heer's desk, where there was a candle.

"This is a forgery," he said.

As he spoke, he waved the paper around and, by accident or design, the flame of the candle set it alight. He held it by one corner and let it burn.

Then he told van Schalkwyk to prepare to leave on the first ship bound for Amsterdam. As van Schalkwyk beat a retreat, Jensen called a guard.

"Take this slave to the female dungeon," he ordered, pointing at me.

"Wait," I cried, "Mijn Heer gave me my freedom before he died."

But Mijn Heer was lying in his grave, and all that remained of his will was a trace of ashes. Jensen laughed at me, a cruel laugh. I exploded. I screamed at him, using words that I had never used before nor since. I saw the anger rise on his face. He ordered the guard out and told Rose to lock the door. Then he grabbed me. I called to Rose for help but she just stood and looked. I cannot tell you what he did to me. The last thing I remember is him telling Rose to unlock the door.

CHAPTER SEVEN

Ama's story

Soon after I was lifted onto the English slave ship *The Love of Liberty,* I saw Tomba for the first time. I didn't know his name then and, of course, I had no idea that he would one day be my husband and your father. He was trussed to the foremast, his arms stretched out and tied to a horizontal spar. Like van Schalkwyk's pictures of Jesus Christ, I thought. Even the loincloth. The sun fell on the man and his body shone with sweat. There were red welts on his black skin. Nearby was an open-topped barrel with a metal ladle hanging from the edge. I rose and walked the few steps to the barrel, a little uncertain on my feet as the ship rolled in the swell. I dipped the ladle into the water and sipped the contents to test it. I drank the rest and filled the ladle again. Then, holding it carefully to stop the water spilling, I raised it to the man's lips. He drank greedily and thanked me silently.

The sweat was running into his eyes. I loosened my cloth

and used the end to mop his face, his neck, his arms, and, gently, his whip-marked torso. Then I wound the cloth around my body again.

"More water?" I asked him in Asante.

One of the whites, whom I came to know afterwards as Fred Knaggs, came from behind me and snatched the ladle from my hand and put it back on the barrel, at the same time abusing me in his language.

I stared at him without expression and returned to my seat. The other women murmured to one another.

Knaggs looked at us, and then, with a flick of his whip, drew blood from the man's chest. The man flinched. Knaggs addressed us, but I must have been the only black person who had any inkling of what he was saying. They had sent an armed expedition ashore, far up the coast, and had captured Tomba and thirty of his followers. Knaggs mocked him, calling him General Tomba.

You will have recognized the name of the ship, *The Love of Liberty*. I had been sold to Captain David Williams, Mijn Heer's good friend.

Now I am going to tell you the whole story of what happened on that ship, but, because we are short of paper, I shall tell you to write down only the parts which concern your father. The rest you will just have to remember.

Captain Williams and his crew regarded Tomba as so dangerous that they kept him in chains in the boys' hold, separated from the other men. The next time I saw him, they had brought him out on deck, as they did once a day, for air and forced exercise. Suddenly, almost as one person, the women around me rose to their feet.

"Tomba, Tomba," they cried.

Tomba, who had been led out shuffling the irons which held his ankles, turned and raised his manacled hands, acknowledging their greetings. He spoke a few words in their language and at once, the guard flicked his whip at him. The women saw the lacerations from the beating he had received and there were cries of angry sympathy. Then the guard forced him to the forecastle, where he and the boys took their food.

This happened every day, so I knew him and his name, but he didn't know me then.

While we were still anchored off Elmina, I managed to send a message to Augusta with a local canoe man, begging her to buy me, but nothing came of it.

Then we sailed the short distance to Cape Coast, where there was a great English slave-trading castle. Again I tried to send a message, this time to the Reverend Philip Quaque. I hoped he would recall our conversation at the wedding and thought he might buy me and employ me to teach the children in his school, but again nothing came of it.

I would not have thought to ask Richard Brew to buy me but, as things turned out, he breathed his last on the very day our ship anchored off Anomabu.

Late that afternoon, while Williams was ashore, drinking at Brew's wake with other slave ship captains, a monstrous cloud, a black tower riven by jagged blades of lightning, descended upon us from the east. The crew drove us into the darkness of the female hold and abandoned us to our fate. The storm seemed to pluck the ship from the surface of the ocean and then plunge it down into the depths, again and again. Inside the hold, we, too, were repeatedly thrown into the air and then dashed down upon the boards, this way and that, until at last, having done its worst, the squall passed on, leaving us to a fitful, painful sleep, a sleep from which eight of us never woke. Perhaps, it struck me later, Brew's spirit, like Osei Kwadwo's, needed an escort to the next world.

When Captain Williams returned to the ship the next morning, he brought his nephew, whom you know, with him.

One Sunday afternoon, sitting amongst the women on the quarterdeck, I heard a harsh, male English voice. Turning, I saw that the man Knaggs and four of his cronies had gathered at the foot of the quarter-deck stairs. I couldn't hear what they were saying, but it seemed clear that they were up to no good. One of the men climbed the steps, looked around, and beckoned to one called Knox to join him. Knox's eyes wandered over the ranks of the women. Some were sleeping, some sitting quietly. I sensed danger. Knox seemed to come to a decision. He pointed to one of the women. Then he and his companion strode across and grabbed her, each taking an arm. Knox stuffed a rag into her mouth to stifle her screams. Some women stood up, alarmed. The sleepers awoke, still not aware of what was happening.

The two white men dragged the woman down the steps and propped her against the main mast. She was wide-eyed with terror. The gag prevented her from crying out, but I sensed her muffled scream as Knox's accomplice twisted her arms behind the mast. Knox fumbled with his trouser cord and then he was inside her. But she twisted to one side and, in that movement, expelled his organ. He took a step back and slapped her face so violently that her head struck the mast. She stopped resisting. Knox re-entered her. His mates cheered.

But even in their excitement, they kept their voices low, looking back at the quarter-deck from time to time. Then Knox made his final triumphant thrust. He withdrew and his accomplice released his hold on the woman. She slumped to the deck and the man dragged her to one side.

"You next, Fred," said Joe Knox, licking his lips as he pulled up his trousers.

All this time, I had been standing, gripping the shrouds of the mizzen mast, unable to act. Now, as Knaggs bounded up the steps, I moved forward, determined to mobilize the other women. If we did nothing to defend ourselves, we would surely be raped one by one, whenever these men chose.

Knaggs was in a hurry. I suppose he was worried that the sudden appearance of the captain or one of his officers might spoil his plans. But he was aroused. His friend Knox had had his satisfaction and nothing would stop Fred Knaggs from having his. He grabbed the first female at hand, a young girl, one of Tomba's people, so young that her breasts were barely formed. I struggled to make my way through the crowd of women. They were protesting noisily but doing nothing else to prevent the outrage. I saw that I would not reach Knaggs in time to try to drag the girl from his clutch.

Without thinking, I called out, "Fred Knaggs!"

He paused, clearly astonished at hearing his name spoken in a female voice.

"Who called me name?" he demanded.

"I did," I said. "Release that girl at once, you scoundrel. You ought to be ashamed of yourself. She is young enough to be your daughter."

For a moment Knaggs seemed immobilized by his astonishment, but he recovered quickly and threw the girl aside.

"Young enough ter be me daughter, are she? But yous ain't then, is yer?" he said.

I was now standing defiantly before him. He grabbed my wrist and dragged me off behind him. He was immensely strong. I felt quite helpless. He forced me up against the mast.

To one of the men who volunteered assistance, he said, "Lay off. Fred Knaggs'll 'andle this un 'isself."

The women were shouting abuse at him, but he paid no attention.

I felt disembodied, as if I were a spirit floating above, watching these events from on high. My mind was sharp. The man was strong but he was foolish, and he could not be aware that this was not my first experience of attempted rape. This time I was determined that things would turn out differently. He leaned his chest against me, panting as he released his trousers. Pinning me to the mast with his left arm thrust against my neck, he sought to guide his organ into me with his right hand.

Mustering all my strength, I drove my knee upwards into his crotch. He staggered back, bellowing with agony. He was doubled up, his trousers around his ankles. Now I was white with anger. I felt my heart pumping. If I had had a knife, I would have driven it into him and ripped his belly open. Seeing he was defenseless, at least for a moment, I took the only chance I had to drive my advantage home. I leave you to guess what I did. All I can tell you is that I have never heard such a scream of pain.

Suddenly there came a loud male voice.

"Knaggs!"

It was the captain.

Knaggs was in no condition to answer. He was down on his knees, holding himself and sobbing. His friends drifted away.

I picked up my cloth and wrapped it round my waist. Stepping around my victim, I started up the steps to the quarter-deck. Captain Williams was standing at the railing. Then I felt my knees buckle under me.

When I came to, I was lying on the floor in the Captain's cabin. The surgeon, whom I already knew as Butcher, was kneeling over me, wiping my face with a damp cloth. The room was small. Above me, I saw the boards of the ceiling; beside me, the legs of a chair and a desk.

"She is coming round," I heard the surgeon say.

Then Williams's red face loomed over me.

"Give her a piece of cloth," he said. "I can't have the wench naked in my cabin."

"Can you sit up?" Butcher asked.

"Here," he said as he helped me to my feet, handing me a folded length of cloth from a pile which stood against the wall. "Wrap this around you."

I did as I was told. Every muscle in my body ached. I lifted the cloth to examine my knees. The skin had been grazed off both.

"Let me clean those wounds," said Butcher.

I winced as he sponged the raw flesh.

Now Williams spoke.

"The men tell me that they heard you speak to Knaggs in English. Is that so?"

I nodded, but said nothing.

"I am sorry about what happened this afternoon. Do you understand me?"

I looked him in the eye and nodded again. He dropped his gaze and fiddled with documents on his desk. I saw paper and quills and ink, a side table covered in charts and instruments, on the wall a brass chronometer and a barometer, and behind glass doors a shelf full of books. I knew all these things from my time with Mijn Heer.

"Knaggs will spend the next month chained to the forecastle deck. The scoundrel has given me trouble since his first day on board. He will have plenty of time to reflect on his sins. And I will see to it that there is no repetition."

He paused and looked up at me.

"Don't you understand me? Why don't you answer?"

I looked him straight in the eye again. Again he found an excuse to avert his gaze. I saw that he was angry but I took my time.

"Captain Williams," I addressed him at last, "don't you recognize me?"

I saw him start. He pursed his brow and looked at me intently, screwing up his eyes as if to see me better.

"You are ...?"

I waited for him to finish, but he just continued to stare at me.

"Mijn Heer called me Pamela. You may remember that you were our guest for dinner one evening."

"Butcher," said Williams, "pull up a chair. Then wait outside."

"Sit down," he said as the surgeon closed the door behind him.

I noticed that he didn't say "please." I sat down. The pain in my knees was worse. I squeezed my leg above the wound.

"I am sorry that I didn't recognize you, but ..."

I completed his sentence in my mind ... all black faces look the same to me.

"I was shocked when I heard that de Bruyn was dead. He must have told you that we were planning to do some business together? Tell me what happened."

"He died," I replied.

I saw him thinking, I know that, stupid, but all he said was, "Of what?"

"The yellow jack."

I would answer his questions if I had to, but I was determined to say as little as possible.

"He was a good friend," Williams mused. "But tell me: how do you come to be here?"

"Mijn Heer made a will, giving me my freedom. Jensen," (I spat the name out) "burned it. He ... he sent me back to the dungeon from which Mijn Heer had taken me. What happened afterwards, Captain Williams, sir, I think you know better than I do."

I bared my breast and pointed to the brand mark. Every black man, woman, and child on that ship bore the scarred imprint of the red-hot branding iron, marking us as the property of Williams's distant, unseen employers.

The captain dropped his eyes. I wrapped the cloth around me and tucked the end in. He pursed his lips and drummed his desktop with his fingers.

"Would you like a drink?" he asked me suddenly. "A little rum or brandy, perhaps?"

Zacharias

"My Mother," I say, "now I have something to tell you. Senhor Gavin Williams owns a ship. It is called *The Love of Liberty*."

"Is he using it to bring slaves from Africa?"

"No. He sends sugar to England and on the return journey, he brings mainly cotton cloth. I know that because it is my work to prepare the customs forms."

"Captain Williams told me that he didn't own the ship," she says. "Perhaps he was lying. Or perhaps he bought it later. It was a wreck when we arrived at Salvador. He had to sell us there to pay for the repairs.

"Senhor Gavin might have inherited *The Love of Liberty* from his uncle. Or perhaps it is a different ship altogether and he just gave it the same name."

Shyly, I ask her, “My Mother, may I see the brand mark?”

She stares at me for a moment with her sightless eyes. Then she draws her cloth down and fingers the scarred imprint on her right breast, two interlocking L’s, with a little “o” between them.

“Have you seen it?” she asks, and secures her cloth just as she must have done in Captain Williams’s presence all those years ago.

“The Portuguese do this to their oxen,” she says.

Ama’s story

We moved slowly along the coast. I was kept busy—I had become Butcher’s interpreter and assistant. I used the opportunity to speak to the men in the holds, those with whom I shared a common language. Tomba, too, got to know me, although we had to communicate by signs.

We came to our last port of call, Accra. When Williams dropped anchor, he found that a war engineered by the English, Dutch, and Danish there had produced a glut of slaves.

Within the space of a week, he was ready to set sail.

We were fed and locked into our holds. I overheard Knox talking as they searched our quarters. The seamen were going ashore for their last carouse before we headed out into the ocean. Williams alone, amongst the officers, would remain on board. He had issued a tot of rum and a pistol, powder, and shot to each of the six crew who had drawn lots to remain on board on guard duty.

The sun set. There was nothing to do in the darkness of that foul hold but sleep.

"Pamela!" Williams shouted.

I woke suddenly, as from a bad dream.

"Where is the wench?" I heard him mutter.

He stood in the doorway, his bulky frame silhouetted against the opening.

"Pamela!" he shouted again.

The women were stirring. I felt embarrassed, humiliated. Uncouth bastard, I thought.

"I'm coming," I called back in something between a whisper and a shout.

His speech was slurred. I could smell the rum. I rubbed my eyes. Then I saw the moon, low and enormous. I went to the rail to get a better view of its elongated reflection moving on the swell. Williams was swearing at the keys as he sought to lock the door of the female hold. I looked around. There was a guard at each hatch cover. Asleep, all three of them. I heard snoring from the quarter-deck and craned my neck. Three more, also asleep. This is our chance, I thought, our last chance.

"Here, let me help you," I told Williams.

"Oh no you don't."

He paused to belch and then continued with his fumbling.

"I know what you're up to. Keys ish for the captain. Only for the captain. Unnershtand?"

For a moment I thought he had read my mind. Then I dismissed the thought. As he turned I saw how drunk he was. I flinched as he groped for my breasts. Then his foul tongue was in my mouth. I freed myself and pushed him away.

"Not here," I whispered. "The guards will see us."

He suffered himself to be led down to his cabin. My mind was racing.

"Lie down," I told him.

When he fell asleep, I covered him with his sheet and sat down in the chair behind his desk, his chair. When he began to snore, I pulled the top drawer open. The candle flickered. My heart pumping, I found his pistol and took the awful thing out. I had never held a gun before. The metal was cold to the touch. I wondered how it worked and whether I could use it to kill him, there and then. I shuddered at the thought and squeezed my eyes shut. When I was calmer, I took his bunch of keys, opened the cabin door and blew the candle out. Leaving, I locked him in.

Alone and afraid, I paused in the shadow of the awning, watching the sleeping guards.

I found the key and opened the door of the female hold. Inside, I paused to recover my calm.

Then I made my way over the naked bodies, searching at every step for a place to put my foot, breathing "Sorry," to the mumbled curses and moving on again.

A narrow beam of moonlight from a vent fell on the door to the boys' hold. I unlocked it and left it ajar. Below, it was dark, pitch dark. I heard the clink of metal.

"Tomba," I whispered, "it is me, Ama."

I hoped that he would recognize my voice even if he couldn't understand the words I spoke.

I heard him sit up. He could not move without rattling his chains. I knelt by his side and let him feel first the bunch of keys and then the gun. I heard the surprise in his grunt.

After what seemed an age, matching a key to the padlock which secured his chains, he was free. He massaged his ankles and his wrists and I heard him wince.

"*Kòse*," I sympathized, knowing how raw his skin was.

He took my hands in his and squeezed them.

"Thank you," he said in his language.

One of the boys, Kofi, a Fante, had picked up a few words of Tomba's language. I would need to use him as an interpreter. I tried to lead Tomba to where the boys were sleeping but he resisted with a vigorous shaking of his head. He led me to the bottom of the stairs and told me to wait. Then he groped his way along the wall to the sick bay. When he came back, there were two men with him. They whispered excitedly amongst themselves.

At the top of the stairs, I took Tomba's hand and signed to him to tuck the gun into his waist-cloth and use his other hand to hold his companion's. So they made a chain and followed me, step by step, across the floor of sleeping women. I set a slow pace. If any of them were to wake, that might be the end. After what seemed to me an age we emerged into the narrow strip of shade under the edge of the quarter-deck.

The moon was higher now, and smaller.

I pointed out the guards sleeping on the hatch covers and showed Tomba the bunch of keys. I pointed up to the quarter-deck and raised three spread fingers. He held up three fingers of each hand. In the moon light I could see that he was asking me to confirm that there were only six guards. I nodded.

I said, "The others," and pointed to the shore.

He thought for a moment and then whispered to his companions, indicating the guards on the hatches as he did so. I thought, it is too dangerous; the others will wake up. I grabbed his arm and shook my head. I tried to tell him by signs that it would be better to capture Williams and use him as a hostage; but the message was too complicated and I could not make him understand. Now he was impatient. If they were to act, they must do so without delay. He signed to me that I should give him the keys and go inside the female hold. I protested vigorously. I had started this thing and I intended to see it through to the end. Tomba whispered to his accomplices and they removed their waist-cloths. He took one and demonstrated what he wanted them to do, wrapping the cloth around the neck of one and twisting it.

The men shook hands. Tomba took my hand and squeezed it.

"Good luck," I whispered. "May the ancestors protect you."

As they tiptoed across the moonlit deck on their bare feet, I mouthed a silent prayer.

"Itsho," I said, "be with them. Guard them. Bring them success."

They paused at the first guard. Tomba left one of his men there. They went on to the second and he left the other. Alone, he went on to the hatch which gave access to the forward hold. Signals passed between them. I dug my nails into my sweating palms. Tomba raised the pistol high in the air and drove it down onto the temple of the sleeping guard. I closed my eyes. When I opened them, Tomba was rolling his victim over and taking his pistol. But the other two victims refused to die without a struggle. Waking to find themselves being strangled, they kicked and fought. Tomba ran across to help.

Suddenly there was a cry from the forecastle, "Wake up! Wake up! Guards, wake up!"

I broke out in a cold sweat. It was Knaggs. I had completely forgotten him. It was my fault. We were undone!

Tomba hesitated. He, too, had forgotten about Knaggs. He turned back to deal with him. Then it must have struck him that Knaggs was chained to the deck and could do no more harm than he had already done. He turned again, to help his co-conspirators.

"Tomba! Unlock the hatch," I shouted but, if he heard, he did not understand.

The three guards on the quarter-deck had run to the barricade. Shots rang out. The slaves might have taken their victims' pistols from them and fired back, but Knaggs's screams from forward and the firing from aft confused them. One of their victims was already dead; the other, free of his assassin's attentions but half-dead from the attempted strangulation, rolled off his hatch cover and lay low. Now it was three against three, but the guards on the quarter-deck had the protection of the barricade and the advantage of elevation. I huddled beside the open door of the female hold, shivering from fear and the chill of the night air.

Tomba took refuge behind the main mast. At best he could fire a single shot with each pistol. The guard who had survived rose to his knees, took his pistol from where it had fallen and crept up behind Tomba.

"Tomba, Tomba," I cried, but it was already too late.

The revolt had failed. It was all over.

Chapter Eight

Zacharias

I don't know what to say. I just don't have words to react to this story. My Mother looks at me with her sightless eyes, the right one just an empty socket.

The eyes of sighted people often send you a message, either supporting the words they speak, or sometimes contradicting them; but the face of a blind person is more difficult to read.

"Kwame, are you there? Have you nothing to say?" she asks.

"Did my father kill that man?" I ask.

"Is that all you have to say?"

I think she expects me to praise their courage, hers and my father's. But if that courage led to the death of an innocent man, what then?

"The Lord has commanded us, 'Thou shalt not kill,'" I want to tell her, but the words stick in my throat.

"Read what you have written," she says. "We still have to deal with what happened next."

Ama's story

The four of us were lined up before tables on which lay the bodies of the two dead white men.

"Before we consign the mortal remains of the unfortunate Hatcher and Baker to the deep," Williams told the crew, "Dr. Butcher will make two incisions in their bodies and extract from each the heart and the liver. Two hearts, two livers. Each of the four criminals will be made to eat one organ."

There was a buzz of conversation amongst the crew. I understood the words but the meaning escaped me. My fellow slaves, understanding nothing, were silent.

"The good doctor tells me," Williams continued, "that this punishment does not conform to the norms of civilized society. I have explained to him that this is not a civilized society. These people are barbarians, devil-worshippers, cannibals. It might well be that consumption of a white man's organs will have some beneficial effect upon them. I have had my say. Mister Butcher, please proceed."

In my worst nightmares, I had never expected this. To be subjected to torture; to be shot or hanged; to be fed alive to the sharks, perhaps. But to be forced to eat human flesh! From where I stood, I could see George Hatcher's face, no longer red, gray now. I was sorry that fate had chosen him to be one of our victims. After Knaggs's attempt at rape, he had talked to me, telling me how he, too, had been forced aboard *The Love of Liberty*, press-ganged. He was a good man, drawn into all this, as I had been, by circumstances beyond his, and my, understanding. Like me, he had a story to tell; but his is lost forever.

I was consumed with a terrible anger at the injustice of life.

"Williams," I screamed, "it is you who are the barbarian, the cannibal. It is you whites who eat the body and drink the blood of your god. It is you who buy human beings and sell them, sell us, as if we were sheep or cattle. It is you ..."

Williams's face turned purple.

"Gag her. Gag her," he screamed.

My words were cut off in mid-sentence as a cloth was stuffed into my mouth.

Butcher finished his operation. Then the two coffins were brought forward. The bodies were put in them and ballast added. The ship's carpenter nailed the lids down.

"Go ahead," Williams told Butcher.

Butcher looked up at him, appealing.

"Do what I say."

The bloody body parts lay on the table.

"I cannot do it," Butcher said, shaking his head.

He seemed close to tears.

Williams looked at him with contempt.

"Knaggs," he called, "come forward."

"You are to feed each of these criminals with one of those organs lying on the table. Do you understand?"

"Yessir. Will they take 'em 'ole or shall I cut 'em up in pieces?" Knaggs asked.

"I leave that to you," Williams replied.

"I think we'll start with Missis Plum Duff," Knaggs said to me. "What'll it be miss, liver or 'eart?"

I remained silent. I had been lucky to win my last clash with this man. Now I was at his mercy. My feet were fettered. My hands were manacled before me. A man had threaded an arm between my elbows and my back. Another held my head immobile. Knaggs cut one of the livers into slices. He held up a piece of the meat between finger and thumb, displaying it to the assembly.

"Let's 'ave no trouble now, miss," he said. "Open yer mouth."

I clenched my teeth. Knaggs put the meat down and tried to force my mouth open. He failed.

"She won' open 'er mouth, sir," he told Williams.

"Butcher," said the captain, "give him your speculum oris."

With a wan look, the surgeon opened his black leather case and took out what looked like an iron scissors.

"Do you know how to use it, Knaggs?" asked Williams.

"Yessir."

He turned a thumbscrew, bringing the two prongs of the

instrument together.

"'Old 'er 'ead firm, now," he told his assistant as he forced the pointed ends between my teeth.

There was a murmur of protest from the men who had been brought out to watch. It was silenced by a threatening flick of the whip. I strained every muscle in my body to resist, but my strength was no match for the three men who now held me. Knaggs turned the thumb screw. The prongs forced my jaws open.

"'Old hit now," said Knaggs, turning to the table.

I had been clenching my muscles tightly against the irresistible force of the speculum. With Knaggs's back turned, I relaxed; then I opened my mouth wide. The instrument fell to the floor. I clenched my teeth again.

There was a cheer from the slaves.

"Knaggs, you idiot," said Williams, "I thought you said you knew how to use the cursed thing."

Knaggs unscrewed the speculum and tried again.

"Go easy, man," said Butcher, "You'll break her jaw."

I closed my eyes. I was on the point of losing consciousness. My head was forced back and I felt the raw meat slither down my throat. Involuntarily, I retched. The piece of liver shot out of my mouth and hit Knaggs in the face. The seamen laughed at his discomfiture. My body sagged and Knaggs's assistants had to hold me up.

"Lay 'er on the deck an' I'll 'ave hanother go," said Knaggs.

"Captain Williams, sir," I heard Butcher say, "surely that is enough?"

Zacharias

My mother has been guilty of the most terrible blasphemy, the way she referred to the Holy Eucharist, but after hearing this story, how can I raise the issue with her now?

"My Mother," I tell her, "I'm sorry."

My words sound so inadequate.

"This all happened many years ago," she says. "The pain has long passed; and yet it is still part of me. And if it is part of me, it is also part of you and part of your daughter Nandzi Ama. This story must not die with me. That is why I have asked you to write it down."

"That Captain Williams," I say. "You said he was the uncle of our Senhor Gavin?"

"Yes," she says.

"And Senhor Gavin was on the ship? Did he see all this?"

"Yes, he was on board and saw it all."

I shake my head in dismay but, of course, she cannot see me.

"But Senhor Gavin is a good man. He is a Christian. How could he have allowed his uncle to do this to you?"

"Kwame," she says, "Miranda has protected you from the harshness of the real world. That is how things are. What, after all, could the Captain's nephew have done? On board a ship, the captain is god. Let us proceed. You haven't heard the end of this story yet."

Ama's story

When I regained my senses, I was propped up against the main mast with my hands manacled behind it.

Tomba lay on the deck before me. The men who had been brought up from the holds as witnesses had turned and were gazing upwards.

Tomba's two accomplices had been trussed, and now they were being hoisted to the lowest yard on the foremast. From the women, there now came a dreadful lament. Determined not to watch the show, I looked straight ahead, blinking the tears away. As my vision cleared, I saw a line of seamen standing behind the barricade on the quarter-deck, each with a musket raised to his shoulder.

"Aim at their hearts," I heard Williams say. "I want no bullets in their heads."

A cry came from the seamen at the foremast, "Ready, Cappin!"

"Hold tight," cried Williams. "Now, men ... ready ... take your aim ... fire!"

Fire and smoke emerged from the barrels of the guns. The crew cheered. The bodies of the victims slumped in their harnesses. From our people, there rose an awful groan. From the holds came an echo of their lament.

The trussed bodies were brought down and laid on the tables, blood dripping from their wounds. I knew that it was now Tomba's turn and mine.

But Williams said, "Firing squad, you may retire."

I thought I had seen a glint of madness in his eye, but his orders were short and precise.

"Knaggs, another job for you. Take the cutlass and decapitate the corpses."

"Sir?"

"Decapitate. Cut off their heads."

Knaggs's eyes opened wide. Then his small brain understood. Holding the cutlass in both hands, he raised it above his head. He turned to look at his fellow seamen. Then he brought the knife down, severing the corpse's neck with a single blow. The head fell to the deck, rolled a short distance, and came to a stop. Blood trickled from each part of the severed neck. Again there came a groan of bottomless despair.

"Good," said Williams. "They are beginning to get the message. And now the other one."

"Well done, Knaggs," he said when the second head lay on the deck. "Now I need another volunteer. You, Knox; you have volunteered. Step forward now."

"Yessir," said Knox.

"You will each take one head. Hold it between your palms like this."

He demonstrated to them. Each man picked up a head.

"Now, Knaggs, you will start from the port side and you, Knox, from starboard. Present your head to each slave in turn. Make them kiss the lips. If force is necessary to achieve this, it will be used. Now proceed."

As Knaggs pressed the head against the face of the first man, forcing him to kiss its lifeless lips, I shouted, "No, no. Don't do it. Do not let them force you."

"That woman is incorrigible. Knox, take the bloody head to her. Now make her kiss it."

I shook my head from side to side, struggling desperately.

"Knox," called Williams, "just press the end of the neck into her face."

Zacharias

I wanted to throw up.

"My Mother," I begged, "please, let us take a rest. It's too much, all at once."

"No," she said, "I want to finish with this now. Today I feel strong. It might not be so tomorrow."

We had a little fire going, just outside her door.

"Is the pot on the fire?" she asked. "I'm thirsty."

While she sipped her maté, I asked her, "My Mother, why did the captain not kill you and my father, too?"

"Tomba was too valuable. Williams must have expected to make a good profit when he sold him."

"And you?"

"Who can see into the mind of a madman? My guess is that he thought that death was too light a punishment for me."

Ama's story

When the obscene kissing was over, Knaggs challenged Knox. Their mates bet their rum allowances on who would win.

At a count of one-two-three, the two men ran to the gunwale and simultaneously threw the heads far out to sea. Time seemed to have stopped. As if in a dream, the heads floated in the air, spinning, so that one moment you saw the face, the next the unkempt hair.

Knox was the winner—his head struck the water further from the ship; Knaggs was in poor condition after the weeks he had spent in irons on the forecastle.

The two headless bodies were unceremoniously dumped overboard for the sharks.

Now Tomba was bound to the foremast. Williams descended to the main deck and swung the cat-o'-nine-tails at his back. He inflicted the same punishment on me. Then he returned to the quarter-deck and watched as each member of the crew took a turn at lashing us. Only Butcher was exempt; his job was to count the lashes, shouting out the number and making a tick in his record book for each.

They took their time. The first lash hurt me most. Some of the knotted ends of the whip drew blood from my back; some wrapped themselves around my body and struck my naked belly and breasts. While I waited I closed my eyes and tried to discipline my mind, forcing myself to concentrate on Itsho, numbing myself to all else. Then, without warning, Knaggs threw a bucketful of sea water over my broken skin. The sting of the salt broke me and I wept.

At every stroke, the watching men and women raised their voices, calling down the wrath of our ancestors and sharing our agony. A moment later, there would be an echo from the holds.

In between the lashes, I was dimly aware of other events. The long boat swung out and the two coffins were lowered into it. A small crew rowed it out to sea. The ship's flag was dropped to half-mast. A seaman blew a tuneless blast on a trumpet, while another beat a monotonous boom-boom-boom on a drum. From the long boat the chief mate gave a signal. Williams read from the Book of Common Prayer. Then he ordered the canons to be fired in honor of the two dead seamen. There were twenty blasts, one for each year of the life of Harry Baker, the age of George Hatcher being unknown. I would have put my hands to my ears, but my hands were not free.

After the burial at sea, the interval between the lashes became shorter. I tried to keep count. I was telling myself, fifty, fifty, fifty, when Knaggs's turn came round again. He twirled the cat and swung high, aiming at my head. One knot tore at my left ear. A bunch struck the back of my head. The knot on the longest strand took out my right eye.

Zacharias

It is Saturday. Josef tells me that we are going to spend the night in the forest. He doesn't tell me why, just to bring my sleeping mat and blanket, a plate, a spoon, and a mug. My mother will be coming, too.

We meet in the dark near the allotments. There is much shaking of hands. I gather that they do this several times a year, but it is a long time since my mother last went. We set off in single file. The dry leaves speak to our bare feet. My mother stumbles behind me, holding on to my backpack with both hands. As soon as we are out of sight of the big house, torches are lit and passed back along the line. Now it is easier for me to follow those ahead of us but, for my mother, the torches make no difference. They start singing quietly, songs that I have never heard before.

The moon has risen when we reach our destination, a clearing in the forest. The women light fires and start to cook. I have never been in the depths of the forest at night before. Beyond the perimeter of the moonlit, torchlit clearing, the darkness strikes me as malevolent, full of sounds I cannot identify. Josef calls me and tells me to take my mother's hand. We follow him and Olukoya and a few others along the side of a shallow stream to another clearing nearby.

A gigantic tree, buttressed by its spreading roots, stands near the center, dominating the open space. Its trunk rises unseen through the darkness, stretching heavenwards. In the dim light, I see that its lower reaches are decorated with white ribbons and flags. The air is quite still.

Silently, we arrange ourselves in a half-circle.

Unseen drummers beat a quiet, gentle rhythm.

Olukoya stands before the tree, barefoot and naked from the waist up. Gazing up into the dark canopy and then down into the shadows behind the roots, he speaks a few sentences in a strange language. Then, to my surprise, my mother steps forward and does the same. I realize for the first time that this is some sort of pagan rite.

I am afraid. I am a Christian. We worship one God. It is a mortal sin to take part in rites like this. This is the work of the Devil. I don't know what to do. I turn my back and, unseen by the others, make the sign of the cross again and again.

Josef steps forward.

"Onyankopon Kwame, creator of all things, lord of the universe; Asase Yaa, spirit of the earth," he says, speaking in Portuguese, "your children greet you. We have come to tell you that we are here. We have brought a visitor from Salvador, Sister Ama's son Kwame. I speak to you in Portuguese so that he may understand. Before dawn tomorrow we shall return to praise your name and to honor the spirits of our ancestors. Tonight we beg you to protect us as we sleep. Protect us from Sasabonsam and all spirits of ill will which may live in this forest. Now we beg your permission to take leave of you. We shall go and come again tomorrow."

The drums signal the end of the brief ceremony. In the gloom, I cross myself again, whisper Hail Mary's and beg forgiveness.

I take my mother's hand to lead her back.

She says, "Kwame, you are shivering. Are you ill?"

I say, "No, it is nothing."

And then I turn on her.

Unable to control my voice, I say, "You have deceived me. You have trapped me, made me commit a mortal sin. My Mother, I am a Christian. Why have you done this to me? You are all pagans, devil-worshippers."

I have been shouting. Now I break down, sobbing. My mother talks to me but I cannot hear what she is saying. Josef takes her hand from mine and leads her away. Olukoya puts his arm around my shoulders. I try to shake him off but he won't let go.

"Kwame, my son," he tells me, "calm down. I am sorry. We should not have brought you here, but your mother insisted, and there would have been no one to stay with you at the Engenho."

We are back at the first clearing. He calls for a bowl of

cachaça and forces me to drink. It burns my throat. I feel the warmth of it in my stomach.

"Come," he tells me, "we need to talk."

We sit facing one another on smooth rocks by the side of the stream.

"Look around you," he says, pointing. "Almost every one of us here was born in Africa, born free. We were all brought to this country by force, against our will.

"Those who brought us here were Christians.

"Like every other African in Brazil, we have been enslaved; and most of the children born to us in this country, *crioulos* like you, have been slaves from birth. Who owns us? Who are our masters? And our mistresses?"

He waits for my answer. I have to say it: "Christians."

"Before your mother lost her sight, she would sometimes read to us from the Christian Bible. Christians claim that what is written there is the word of God, the god of the Christians. Yet she found there passages justifying slavery. So the Portuguese believe that their god has authorized our enslavement.

"Many years ago, in the time of the old Senhor, there was a priest living here. Father Isaac was his name. His homilies exhorted us to be hardworking, loyal and obedient to our masters, and to suffer our servitude meekly. He supported each admonition with a verse from the Bible. That is the Christianity we know.

"I have never met, in Africa or Brazil, any black man or woman who does not believe in God, whatever name we give him. We come to this forest from time to time to worship our god in the different ways we remember from our own people in Africa. It is a comfort to us. The words we use are full of poetry; the music we play to accompany our prayers is our own music, played on instruments that we ourselves have made. Whatever the Christians tell you, there is nothing sinful or evil about our worship.

"That is all I have to say to you, my son. Do you have any questions?"

I shake my head. I must not reply. An inner voice warns me that the Evil One has taken on the guise of Olukoya, speaking sweet words to undermine my faith. I concentrate my mind on a vision of Our Lord Jesus in the desert, resisting temptation.

"Come with us tomorrow. You need not participate. Just listen and watch," I hear Olukoya say.

The cachaça puts me to sleep. I dream of a man and a boy. They are in a forest. The man is teaching the boy how to set a fish trap; they sit side by side on the bank of the stream, on smooth rocks, fishing. The boy catches his first fish.

On Sunday afternoon my mother is exhausted. When she has fallen asleep in her cabin, I ask a lad for directions to the chapel. I find it, but the door is locked.

CHAPTER NINE

Zacharias

I tell my mother that our stock of paper is running low. She says to stop writing and just listen. She tells me about the rest of their journey in Captain Williams's prison ship, *The Love of Liberty.*

"For weeks and weeks," she says, "we lay becalmed in the middle of the ocean."

Food and water ran low, and every day more slaves were thrown overboard, dead, "to feed the sharks," she says.

She says that once she had made a partial recovery from the whipping, she vowed that she would never again speak to a white man, but that Senhor Gavin ("your Senhor Gavin," she calls him) broke her resolve by reading aloud to her.

"What did he read?" I ask her.

"I forget," she says. "Some English novel. *Tom Jones*, perhaps. Have you read *Tom Jones*? Senhora Miranda told me once that *Tom Jones* was her favorite."

I tell her that the only book I read these days is the Holy Bible. She says she knows it well, in English and in Portuguese. She says that when she has finished telling me her story, I should read the Book of Ruth to her. I may not be able to do that. I have only brought the New Testament with me.

Then she tells me how a great storm in the Atlantic broke the main mast of their ship and drove it into Salvador.

"São Salvador da Bahia de Todos os Santos, the city of the Holy Savior of All Saints Bay," she says. "Your city."

Ama's story

With the crippled ship at anchor in the bay, they brought us soap and buckets of hot water. Soap, mind you, and fresh water, not sea water. They gave us more food and the quality improved. They let us shave our heads. For the first time since leaving Elmina, I was free of lice. They gave us palm oil to rub into our skin and returned our own old cloths to us and let us wash and iron them. I began to feel human again, but I was haunted—we all were—by a sense of foreboding.

After ten days, they ferried us ashore, all of us, women and men. I was with the boy Kofi and his mother. I remember our being led in procession down a long, narrow street, the Rua São Pedro (do you know it?), at the end of which there was a large stone building. When we reached it, Captain Williams and Dr. Butcher stepped out of the *cadeira* in which they had been riding. An official in a fancy uniform was waiting for them. We followed them up a flight of steps into a spacious hall. As the last of us marched in, the great wooden doors closed behind us with a resounding bang. I clapped my hands to my ears. Since the canon of Elmina and *The Love of Liberty*, I have always hated loud noises.

Feeling confused and giddy, I closed my eye and stood quite still. Someone pushed me and spoke harshly. It was a black man. I noticed that he was wearing boots, and that he wasn't averse to using them. I know now, as you do, too, that we slaves are not allowed to shoe our feet, so this one must have been a free man.

He herded us like sheep, pushing and pulling and abusing us loudly in a language none of us understood. I suppose it was Portuguese.

I looked around, trying to get my bearings. Four massive columns rose to support a dome, unlike anything I had seen before. High windows lit the square hall.

Ushers shepherded us into the central arena and forced us to sit down, facing outwards. Williams and Butcher and two other white men watched from a platform on one side. When they were satisfied with the arrangements, the two strangers led Williams and Butcher on an inspection. Together, they counted each one of us and, as they did so, an usher hung a board with a chalked number around that person's neck.

I twisted my board and read the number: 117.

I had become separated from Kofi and his mother. On my right sat one of Tomba's womenfolk, a stranger. Though it was hot, the woman was shivering. I took her hand and spoke to her.

Trying to comfort myself, I told her, "My sister, everything will be all right."

The woman squeezed my hand.

I looked to my left. Sitting two men away was Tomba himself. He had been watching me. He smiled. Then he showed me a clenched fist. It was our first communication since the rebellion.

He put his finger to his right eye and shook his head sadly.

I mouthed a silent reply, knowing he would understand: "It is nothing. It was not your fault."

The bells of a nearby church rang out. As the last echo died away, a band of barefooted black musicians began to play fiddles, guitars, and drums. Then the doors were opened once more. A crowd of men, mainly white, but with a sprinkling of mulattos and blacks, poured into the room.

A large signboard showed the day's asking price: 120 milréis. The purchasers strolled around, viewing us and making notes. A customer called out in Portuguese, pointing to a man sitting behind me. An usher prodded him and pushed him forward to allow the senhor to take a closer look.

The music stopped. Outside the hall, a man's loud sing-song voice called out the same word over and over again, accompanied by the jingling of a bell.

"*Escravos, escravos.*"

That was the first Portuguese word I learned.

The crowd of buyers and spectators thickened. The hall began to fill with the smoke of many pipes.

Now it was Tomba's turn. He refused to rise and two ushers had to force him to his feet. They held him, one at each arm.

"Tomba, Tomba," I called, "it is no use fighting here. You cannot win."

An old man extended his stick and tapped the muscles of Tomba's arm. He turned and nodded his approval to one of the slaves who accompanied him, a gray-bearded black man, as old as he, neatly dressed, but barefooted. Then he pointed with his stick to the cloth which Tomba wore around his waist. Before Tomba knew what was happening, one of the ushers had grabbed the cloth, leaving him naked. Tomba swore violently and struggled to free himself, but the ushers knew their job. Calmly the old man extended his stick and used it to lift Tomba's penis, adjusting his monocle with his free hand. Then, without another look at Tomba or the ushers, he passed on to the next slave.

Tomba recovered his cloth and turned on the ushers. I saw the hatred and contempt in his eyes. They ignored him. He sank to his knees, elbows and forehead on the floor, his head grasped in his hands.

"Tomba," I called to him, "bear up. It is all right. We are all in this together."

Once they had completed their inspection, the purchasers made their payments to the clerks, who issued a numbered token for each one hundred and twenty *milréis* paid. The total number of tokens sold so far was marked up on a chalkboard, together with the number of us slaves on offer. Some buyers wandered back to take another look at us, pointing out their preferences to their agents or employees. Others sat with the drinks which were on offer and chatted quietly or just listened to the music. We sat and waited, scared, unable to guess what would happen next.

At last an announcement was made. The ushers forced us to our feet and drove us to the center of the hall. Some marched around us, threatening any who were stupid or brave enough to resist. We huddled together. The purchasers took up positions on a line which had been painted on the floor from column to column.

I saw them fiddling with lengths of ribbon and handkerchiefs knotted end to end. Kofi pushed his way through the crowd to greet me.

"Kofi," I told him urgently, "go straight back to your mother and stay with her. Hold her tight. Do not let go of her."

As I was saying this, the trumpet player blew a fanfare. In the ensuing silence, the master of ceremonies spoke a few words in Portuguese. I saw the buyers stiffen. Then there came a short count, followed by the single shrill blast of a whistle.

At that signal, the buyers rushed at us. There was pandemonium. Some of our men stood firm, ready to fight. The band blasted out on its trumpets and drums; buyers shouted. Some of our women and children shrieked in terror.

The enemy was upon us, grabbing at our arms, our cloths, pulling us to one side, throwing us down to the ground, tying us with their ribbons and handkerchiefs.

Suddenly, almost as suddenly as it had started, it was all over. Only the few stragglers who had paid for five and only managed to capture four were heard to complain as they sought to identify those who had grabbed more than their fair share.

The band played soothing music, strings. One of the musicians sang a plaintive song.

"Kofi, Kofi," I heard a desperate cry.

I found myself in a group of ten, some of whom I knew by sight, but none well. Tomba was not amongst them. My good eye searched the little groups, but I could see no sign of him.

Our herder, a black man, fussed over us. Apprehensive that we might try to run off, he forced us to sit on the floor. The two other women amongst us were sobbing. A man sank his head between his knees.

Then the white master appeared and spoke to his black minion.

"Roberto," I heard him call.

Roberto ordered us to stand. First he spoke Portuguese, but it was clear that none of us understood.

"*Mónsoré*-o, get up, get up," he tried in Asante.

Uncertain, a man rose. I did so, too, and the rest followed our example.

"Brother, you speak Asante?" I asked Roberto.

"Don't call me brother, woman. I am not an unseasoned guiney bird like you. Now, stand in a line so that master can look at you properly."

The master examined and counted us. He seemed satisfied with his prize.

"*Vamos. Mma yeñkô*. Let's go," Roberto told us.

At the door we paused. A clerk checked us off against our new owner's tokens and recovered our chalk boards.

I caught a last glimpse of Captain Williams, glass in one hand, cigar in the other, in earnest conversation with Butcher. And then I was blinded by the bright sunlight.

Zacharias

She tells me how Josef collected her from a slave merchant in Salvador and brought her across the bay in the old Senhor's boat. The old Senhor, who bought her, died years ago. He was Senhora Miranda's father. At that time she understood no Portuguese, so it was a great comfort to her, she says, that she and Josef had a language in common. She tells me of the years she worked in the fields, back-breaking work, loading sticks of sugar cane onto the ox-carts. When she begins to tell me about her work in the mill, I interrupt her. I have seen the hell of the sugar mill with my own eyes and I have no wish to be reminded of it.

She agrees.

"Now I must explain how I came to be transferred to the casa grande," she says.

"I would like to hear that," I say. "Shall I write this down? I still have a few pages to fill."

Ama's story

There was a vacancy. One of the house slaves had died in childbirth. This time, the old Senhora was determined not to recruit another candidate for the bed of the old Senhor, who had so often in the past been the agent of her shame.

She told Jesus Vasconcellos, the manager, "Bring me the six ugliest wenches you have."

Of course, the news got round; there are few secrets at the Engenho de Cima. When I learned that my name was on the short-list of the ugly, I felt crushed. I ran to my cabin, buried my head under my blanket, and cried until I could cry no more. I suppose it was vanity. Men had admired me—two kings of Asante and a Dutch governor, amongst them. Now I had to come to terms with my disfigured appearance.

Jacinta, who shared my cabin and who had lost both her

lower arms in an accident in the mill, tried to console me.

"Look at me," she said, holding up her stumps.

But that only set me off on a fresh fit of sobbing.

Then old Benedito took up his Christian duty and came to visit me, misquoting Ecclesiastes on vanity. I bit my tongue, thanked him with the humility and respect due to his years, and sent him on his way.

It was Wono, Josef's wife, who at last brought me to my senses.

"Don't be stupid, sister Ama," she said. "After all, who cares about what Vasconcellos or the other whites think? In a way, you are lucky—at least Senhor Jesus might keep his hands off you if that is what he thinks. And if the Senhora selects you, just think, you will be better fed and better clothed and you won't have to work so hard. What is more, you will keep us informed about what is going on up there."

Now I must tell you how ... no, let the story speak for itself.

Late one night, Josef returned from Salvador.

The next morning, he brought the mail to the kitchen and I took it out to the Senhor with his breakfast tray.

He glanced at the first letter.

"Girl, what's-your-name?" he said. "Go and call Father Isaac and tell him I want to speak to him. Father Isaac, the priest. Do you understand?"

I said I understood. By that time I had mastered Portuguese.

"Sit down, Father," the Senhor said when the priest came. "Girl, pour the Father a cup of coffee."

"Father, do you know any English?"

"English? No, Senhor," Father Isaac replied. "Latin, yes. A little Spanish, but no English. If I may ask, Senhor, why?"

"Look at this letter from the Governor. The English Consul in Salvador wants to do me the honor of being my guest. His Excellency has authorized the visit. There is no way I can refuse. Please draft a reply for me to sign. Tell them that he will be welcome but that there is no one here who understands the man's language. If he does not speak Portuguese, he will have to bring an interpreter with him."

Please Senhor, I imagined myself saying, there is no need. I know English well. I could act as the Consul's interpreter if you would permit me to do so. But, of course, I held my tongue.

"What does it say? When will he be arriving?" the Senhor asked.

"Next Friday, subject to your agreement," Father Isaac replied.

"Make a list. We'll invite all our neighbors to a banquet on Saturday night. And their wives, too. They can sleep over and attend Mass on Sunday. You would like that, wouldn't you?"

He rubbed his hands together.

"We'll show this Englishman the meaning of Brazilian hospitality," he said.

Additional slaves were brought in to help with the preparations. The seamstresses worked long hours, repairing the uniforms of those who would wait at table. The best plate and silver was washed and polished. Linen was aired and ironed. Bernardo, the Fante carpenter, made new beds. Even the workers in the mill and in the cane fields felt the excitement. It was almost as if the expected visitor were the Governor of all Brazil himself.

I was kept busy in the kitchen. I hadn't seen so much food since Kumase. Wono was there, too. And Josef would be serving at table.

The Senhora was flustered.

"We are short one server," she said. "Ama, do you think you could manage?"

"Of course, Senhora. At least, I shall do my best."

"I hope the guests won't be frightened by your bad eye; but there is no one else. Go to the seamstresses and get yourself fitted."

Wono took my hands and we did a little dance together.

When the English Consul arrived, I was in the sewing room, trying on my new dress. It was the fanciest garment I had worn since Mijn Heer's death.

The dining room was ablaze with the light of a hundred candles and oil lamps.

On the brilliant white table cloth, the silver and plate and glassware glittered and gleamed. Around the walls stood sixteen barefooted slaves, one behind each chair, the men in smart livery and the women, including me, in full petticoats. Two *crioulos* in a corner played fiddle and guitar.

The Senhor led in the beautiful young wife of a neighboring senhor de engenho. She wore a dress of green damask and silk which took my breath away. Slaves stepped forward to pull their chairs.

I turned to look at the next couple and suddenly felt faint. The Senhora was clutching the arm of none other than ... Kwame can you guess?

Zacharias

Sometimes my mother treats me as if I were still a child.

I don't have to guess. I have listened to Senhora Miranda tell her daughter, Senhorita Elizabeth, about this dinner party, not once but many times. Elizabeth always complains that she has heard the story before and doesn't need to hear it again.

"It's so boring," she says.

But I would never speak to my mother as Elizabeth speaks to hers, so I humor her.

"Let me think," I say. "Was it by any chance Senhor Williams? I mean my Senhor Williams as you call him, the nephew not the uncle."

"How clever of you," she says. "It was indeed Gavin

Williams, the nephew of the captain of *The Love of Liberty*."

Ama's Story

Could it really be him? I wondered. He was deep in conversation with the Senhora, Portuguese conversation. Ignoring the slave whose duty it was, he pulled back the Senhora's chair at the foot of the table. Then Williams took his own seat, next to the beauty in green who sat in the place of honor on the Senhor's right.

Miranda came in last, on the arm of Father Isaac. She was wearing a modest white organdie dress which I had helped to make. The priest led her to her seat on her father's left, where he could keep an eye on her. This was the first time she had been permitted to attend an adult function. I could sense just how nervous she was as I drew her chair for her.

Father Isaac rose and said grace. When the guests had added their amens, we stepped forward to serve them, one of us for each guest. I poured red wine into Miranda's glass. As I did so, Williams noticed me. He might have been struck first by my missing eye. Then he took another look and at once, he knew me. He sat back in his chair and stared. I put down the bottle and retired to my position behind my young mistress. I raised my head, returning his stare, but giving no indication that I recognized him as anything other than just another visiting white man.

"Just a sip, now," the Senhor admonished his daughter.

"Senhor Gavin, this is my daughter, the apple of my eye."

"Of course, Senhor, the good Father introduced us. Senhorita Miranda, if I am not mistaken? A young woman, if you will permit me to say so, Senhor, of remarkable beauty."

Miranda blushed and the Senhor smiled.

A silent signal sent me to the kitchen. When I returned with a tureen of steaming turtle soup, Williams was deep in conversation with his host.

"Senhor," he asked, "how long has this engenho been in your family?"

"Twenty-five years," replied the old man. "It used to belong to the Jesuits. When they were sent packing in 1759, the government sold it by auction. Mine was the best offer."

One course followed another: first fish from the bay, grilled over charcoal; next, a seafood stew with okra and palm oil; then chicken cooked in blood.

I was astonished at the amount they were able to consume.

Two of our men brought in a spit-roast suckling pig on a great platter. The guests applauded. The men carried it round the table for all to see and then took it aside to carve it.

The food these sixteen are eating in one sitting, even the leftovers on their plates, would last us all a week, I thought.

In between my trips to the kitchen, I caught snatches of conversation. The Senhor was flattered by Williams's questions and held forth at great length on the problems of the sugar trade; on the extortion practiced by priests of the Santa Casa da Misericórdia, the only money-lenders in Bahia; and on the corruption of government officials in Salvador.

"Every one loveth gifts, and followeth after rewards," Father Isaac said, beginning to slur his words.

Williams penciled a note in the small book he kept by his side.

The Senhor paused to do justice to the chicken.

"This fowl is delicious," said Williams. "Senhora, please accept my compliments on your magnificent cuisine."

The Senhora blushed and bowed her head in acknowledgement. Miranda blushed in sympathy.

It struck me that none of the women had said a word.

Zacharias

Senhora Miranda's version revolves around Senhor Gavin. She says he couldn't keep his eyes off her right through that meal. She told that story once when he was present, and he just smiled. My mother's version doesn't contradict Senhora Miranda's, and yet the picture it brings to my mind is quite different. One event, two reporters: whose story is the more reliable? Human memory is fallible. If I were to question the accuracy of my mother's account, would she be offended? I wonder.

When I return to Salvador, I'll ask Senhor Gavin to tell me his version of how my mother lost the sight of her eye.

Ama's story

The Senhor sat on his veranda. He had overslept and missed morning prayers again.

A full week had passed since the dinner party. The Brazilian guests had stayed just long enough to attend a late Mass.

Only the Englishman lingered on at the Engenho, riding the Senhor's stallions down to the cane fields; studying the work in the mill; inspecting our senzalas and allotments. And always asking questions and making notes in his little book.

I came out with the breakfast tray. On the steps, Alexandré, Miranda's mulatto half-brother, whittled away at a piece of soft wood. He peeped at the Senhor, but knew better than to attempt to talk to him so early in the day.

"Senhor," I said, "I beseech your blessing in the name of our Lord and Savior Jesus Christ."

The Senhor grunted what might have been a blessing but might just as well have been a curse. He was always cool toward me. He had never had an African as a house slave before. I had heard him say that he preferred mulattos, or at least *crioulos*. We Africans were not to be trusted—we were too proud and rebellious. He asked his wife why she had brought this one, that is, me, into the *casa grande*; and why she had done so without consulting him beforehand. He complained that his authority was being undermined. Everyone seemed to be taking advantage of his advancing years.

I stole a sidelong glance at the Senhor as I put down the tray. He was usually in a bad temper at this time of the morning, particularly when he had drunk too much the night before. His face was unshaven. Strands of white hair lay untidily across his red pate. I wondered whether he was upset that Williams had defeated him at chess the previous day. I had noticed that Father Isaac took great pains never to beat the Senhor.

"Will there be anything more, Senhor?" I asked.

I took his grunt to mean "no" and retired to the back of the veranda, out of his sight but ready to react to his slightest gesture or command, as I had been taught. But I was tired. They had kept me up late several nights running. I let my back slide slowly down the wall until I was sitting on the stone floor. I hugged my knees to my chest and dozed.

"A very good morning to you, Senhor," I heard Williams say. "May I join you?"

I wondered whether I should get up to pour coffee for him, but he was already helping himself.

"Thank you for the chess last night. I really did enjoy it."

I laughed inwardly at the Englishman's attempts to draw a reply out of the Senhor. I stretched forward so that I could see them.

"Senhor. There is an important matter which I should like to discuss with you. Could we talk now or would another time be more convenient?"

The Senhor shifted his weight in his chair and took a deep breath.

"Speak, Senhor Gavin. There is no time like the present."

There was an awkward pause. Williams was folding and refolding his handkerchief.

At last he summoned up his courage.

Looking straight ahead, he said quietly, "It is about your daughter, Senhorita Miranda."

I peeped out again. The Senhor was cutting himself a cigar. It was unusual for him to smoke so early in the morning.

One of the overseers trotted up on a horse.

"Later, later," the Senhor dismissed the man.

Then he saw his bastard son sitting on the steps.

"Alexandré," he said. "Shove off!"

"What about Miranda?" he asked when the boy had gone.

"It's no use beating about the bush," Williams replied. "She won my heart the moment I first set eyes on her. I want to ask your permission ..."

He looked up. The Senhor was staring into the distance.

"Your permission ... Senhor, I hope I haven't offended you."

"Have you spoken to her about this?"

"No, no, we have hardly exchanged half a dozen words all the time I have been your guest. And those were mere pleasantries, hardly even a conversation. Senhor, I hope

I haven't stepped out of line in speaking to you as I have. I know that ..."

"Senhor Gavin, you are a Protestant."

"Oh, that would not present a problem. I could become a Catholic if that were your wish."

"You are an Englishman."

"Welsh, actually," Williams replied. "There is nothing I can do about that, I'm afraid."

"You would take my only daughter away from me."

"Not while you live, sir. Not while you or the Senhora is alive. That I promise. That I swear."

They went on talking—questions, answers, promises.

My one eye was wide open and my ears, too. I wanted to get away and tell someone the news, tell Miranda, tell anyone. But how could I escape without them noticing me? Williams, at least, would know that I had heard and understood. As for the Senhor, he thought that slaves' ears had no function beyond the receipt of commands.

"Senhor Gavin, I will speak to my wife. I make no promises, no commitments. You should on no account discuss this matter with my daughter unless and until you have my consent to do so. Do you understand?"

"Of course."

"We will talk again presently. And tonight, I will avenge my defeat on the board."

Chapter Ten

Ama's story

When I reached the Senhora's quarters, I found Alexandré swinging Miranda round and round at arm's length so that all the furniture was in danger of being toppled over.

Dearly beloved Miranda, Alexandré's elder sister, his half-sister, the apple of their father's eye.

"Senhora Williams, Senhora Williams, Senhora Williams. Say a mass for Saint Gonçalo for finding you a husband," he teased her.

Miranda screamed in mock fear, blissfully ignorant of what he was talking about.

"Alexandré, stop that this minute," I told him.

He let go of Miranda. She stumbled around drunkenly until the dizziness wore off. Then she collapsed in a heap on the floor.

"Alexandré," I reprimanded him, "you have been eavesdropping again."

"Eavesdropping? Me? Ama, I thought you were my friend.

Why do you make false accusations which will get me into trouble? Eavesdropping on whom?"

"Why were you calling Senhorita Miranda Senhora Williams?"

"Oh, that!" he replied.

"Yes, that! You were eavesdropping on the Senhor's conversation with Senhor Gavin, weren't you?"

Alexandré pouted and said nothing.

"What is this all about, Ama?" Miranda asked.

"Senhorita Miranda, can you keep a secret?"

"Of course. Tell me, tell me. What is it all about?"

"If you give me away, the Senhor will send me back to the cane fields."

"I promise. Cross my heart and hope to die."

"This morning I took the Senhor's breakfast tray to him on the veranda. Then I waited in case he needed anything. I was tired and I sat down next to the cabinet. Senhor Williams came out to join your father. He asked for permission to discuss something very important with him."

"This doesn't sound interesting. They are always talking business. Something about the Engenho, no doubt. Why are you telling me this?"

"Young lady, you are too impatient. The important matter Senhor Williams wanted to discuss with your father was ... you."

"Me?"

"Yes, you."

"What have I done now? I have hardly spoken to the visitor."

"Can't you guess?" Alexandré chipped in.

"Alexandré, be quiet," I scolded him. "This is serious. Now listen carefully, Senhorita, and brace yourself for a shock. Senhor Williams was asking your father for permission to court you."

"To court ...?"

Miranda's eyes and mouth opened wide. Then she blushed deeply.

"He wants to marry you."

A tear descended from each of Miranda's eyes. Then she began to sob. I put my arm around her shoulder.

"Don't cry. It is nothing to cry about. He is a fine man. You should be flattered."

That only made things worse. Miranda bawled. She hugged me and sank her head into my breast. I did my best to comfort her.

The door opened and the Senhora entered.

"What's going on in here? The Senhor is complaining about the noise. He has a headache."

Then she saw her daughter crying.

"Miranda, my child, what is the matter? Why are you crying? Alexandré, have you been teasing her again?"

Miranda looked up, speechless, and shook her head. I

moved aside. The Senhora took her daughter's hands.

"There now. Surely it can't be bad enough to make you cry like that?"

Miranda burst into tears again.

"Ama, what is it? Do you know?"

I was silent.

You should have kept your big mouth shut, you stupid slave, I thought. Now you are in real trouble.

Miranda looked up and wiped her face with her hand. Her mother helped her with a handkerchief.

"Tell her," Miranda ordered me.

"Senhorita, you promised."

"Tell her. I promise you on my honor that my father will not send you back to the cane fields."

"Well?" asked the Senhora, losing patience.

There was nothing for it; I had to tell her.

"Senhora, Senhor Williams, the Englishman ..."

"Yes? What about him? Speak, girl, or I'll have you given a good beating."

"He has asked the Senhor for permission to pay court to Senhorita Miranda."

Zacharias

"My Mother," I say, "that is your story. You are the only one who saw and heard it all, the conversation between Senhor Gavin and the old Senhor, Alexandré's mischief, and Senhora

Miranda's reaction when she heard your secret."

"Kwame, you are right. And because of that, in my own foolish way, I have always felt some sort of ownership of their courtship and marriage."

I wonder what Senhor Gavin and Senhora Miranda would think if they knew what my mother was telling me. I'm quite sure Senhorita Elizabeth would be furious. I don't understand why that girl resents me so much. Could it be because, like her parents, I am happily married, while she hasn't been able to find a man good enough to be her husband?

Ama's story

The Senhor gave his consent to Williams's courtship of Miranda.

For practical reasons, he sent her and her mother to stay in the town house in Salvador. Miranda begged her father to join them, but the Senhor was wedded to the Engenho and too lazy to make a move.

I had become Miranda's favorite companion. She wanted to take me to Salvador as her personal maid. I was thrilled at the prospect. But the Senhor vetoed the plan. There was no way he would permit himself to be made a laughing stock in the city, he said. Employing a one-eyed maid to serve his daughter! Williams was a good match for his daughter and he did not intend to allow the Englishman to slip through his fingers. So Miranda gave in and I stayed behind.

Miranda had more success in persuading her father that Alexandré should go with them. The Senhor decided that it was time to send the boy to the seminary in Salvador to prepare him to take holy orders.

Weeks passed. Josef brought regular news. Williams had been received into the Catholic Church. He dined regularly with the Senhora and her daughter. He showered Miranda with exquisite gifts. He escorted them to Mass every Sunday. He took them out driving in his coach.

It was still too early for him to make a formal proposal, but the Senhora had sufficient confidence in his honorable intentions to start assembling her daughter's trousseau. Orders were sent to Lisbon.

Then the Engenho do Meio, the one down the road, was sold. The new owner came to call on the Senhor. He brought in many new slaves. Josef's friend Fifi was made a senior driver by virtue of his local knowledge. Josef rejoiced for him and his family. They had been living in abject poverty. Now things might be a little better.

Williams returned to the Engenho de Cima to make a formal proposal of marriage to the Senhor. A day in June was fixed for the wedding. The Senhor's two elder sons arrived at the Engenho, together with their wives and children, and began to make preparations. The house was too small to accommodate all the guests who were expected.

The neighboring senhores de engenho would help, but tents would also be required, and a grand marquee for the reception. The sons arranged to borrow carriages and ox-carts and boats. They auditioned the slaves who could play musical instruments and sought out others in the neighborhood. The Senhor decided to shut down the mill for a month at the end of the *safra*. His sons needed the extra labor.

So we, a hundred slaves, men, women, and children, devoted all our energies for four weeks to the preparations for the festivities. There would be horse racing and cock fighting, hunting and cards to amuse the men. And eating and drinking, of course. On the night of the wedding, there would be a great ball with an orchestra brought all the way from Salvador. The annual issue of clothes to us was postponed until the eve of the wedding. Each male field hand would receive a pair of drawers that reached below the knee, a coarse homespun shirt, and a bright head kerchief; each woman, a shift, a frock, and an apron; and each child a shirt with long tails. And as a bonus, a new tin plate, a spoon, and a mug.

The Senhor issued instructions that no effort or expense should be spared.

A week before the date set for the wedding, Miranda and her mother returned.

Senhor Gavin came with them and went to stay as the

guest of the new owner of the Engenho do Meio.

As the big day approached, the pace of work quickened. The glamour and excitement of it all affected us, too. The Bishop arrived from Salvador, his throne borne aloft on a litter and escorted by a retinue of his personal slaves. We gathered to watch the family and the visitors line up to kiss his ring. As each party of guests arrived, the Senhor came out to welcome them formally. The yard was full of fine carriages, seldom used because of the condition of the roads. Strange horses raced up and down the paddocks. The estate was alive with strangers. They inspected the livestock and the mill. Some of them even toured the senzalas, poking their heads inside our cabins. The young men regarded us, the female slaves, as fair game, squeezing breasts and pinching buttocks. I found my missing eye a valuable weapon. Assaulted in this way, I gave the assailant a fierce look and spat on the ground. My victim told his fellow rakes that I had the evil eye and they gave me no more trouble.

The unmarried sisters of these young men were kept in seclusion in the Senhora's quarters. Their time would come with the grand ball, an occasion to put their virtuous gifts on display for the benefit of prospective suitors.

We had our own guests to accommodate and entertain, for every white family brought with it a retinue of domestic slaves.

"Maybe we can find you a husband, too, Ama," Wono

teased me.

At ten o'clock precisely (more or less) on the big day, the bridegroom arrived.

A great cheer rose from the guests on the veranda as Williams's carriage approached. It was drawn by four magnificent white mares and escorted by an honor guard of the younger male guests on horseback.

Fifi, dressed in a red uniform with gold braid, held the reins. Beside him, bolt upright, sat a stranger in similar attire.

"Look at Fifi," I said, clutching Wono's arm. "Doesn't he look grand?"

"Who is that beside him?" Wono asked.

"It must be one of the new slaves at Fifi's place," I said.

"Fifi, Fifi," cried Wono, as if it were he who was the center of all this pomp, rather than his passenger.

I looked again at the new man.

"Wono," I said, digging my nails into the flesh of her arm.

"What?" she asked.

"I know him. He was my *malungo* on *The Love of Liberty*."

And then I must have fainted.

When I came to, I was lying in the shade of a tree.

Wono was kneeling by my side. We were surrounded by a crowd of friends.

"Move away, move away," I heard Wono say. "Give her some air."

I opened my eye and blinked.

"What happened?" I asked.

"You fainted," Wono replied. "Are you all right now? Can you sit up? You gave me a quite a start. For a moment I thought you were ..."

"Dead? Me? Not yet, sister Wono."

"Ah, here they come," said Wono.

"Who?" I asked, sitting up.

"Fifi and Josef. And Fifi's friend, your *malungo*. I sent for them."

I felt my heart pumping. I struggled to get up but I was too weak.

"Wono, help me," I begged.

Josef asked, "Wono, what is the matter? The lad you sent sounded anxious."

I said, "It is nothing, Bra Josef. We just wanted to greet Fifi in his fine clothes."

Fifi greeted me in Fante, "Sister Ama, *maakye*. How are you?" and shook hands.

When I had replied, he said, "As for these clothes, they dress us up like performing monkeys when it suits them. I would be happier in my working shirt, hot and itchy as it is. But I forget myself. I haven't introduced our new brother. João, this is Wono, Josef's wife. And this is Ama."

Wono was about to say something but my look shut her up.

I turned and looked Tomba straight in the eye. His mouth opened wide. I would never let him forget the astonishment with which he recognized me. Recovering quickly, he took both my hands in his.

"Sister Ama and I," he said to his new friends in Portuguese, "have met before."

Zacharias

Tomba! My father! He hasn't been far from my thoughts since my mother told me the story of the failed revolt on board *The Love of Liberty*. I have struggled to summon up a picture of him, but in vain. At first I condemned him as a murderer but since then, I have had second thoughts. If a son cannot forgive his own father, who can? Except the Lord, that is.

I need to think about this.

"My Mother," I tell her, "my hand is sore from all the writing and it will soon be dark."

"Tomorrow," she says. "Let us continue tomorrow."

I leave her and take the path behind the *senzalas*, the slave quarters. Halfway up the hill, there is a rocky platform. I sit down and watch the ever-changing chiaroscuro of crimson and gold in the western sky.

"Lord, I see your work," I whisper, and the anger which has threatened to split my brain begins to subside.

I sink to my knees and say the Pater Noster, slowly,

concentrating on each line, praying to the Holy Spirit for the gift of forgiveness.

When I awaken, night has fallen. No moon. No stars. But the hellfire of the furnaces, the terrible handiwork of man, illuminates the mill in the dark valley below.

The rock I have been lying on is damp and my body is sore. I feel my way down the track, back to my room.

Ama's story

Our wedding was celebrated in a more modest fashion than Williams's and Miranda's.

Tomba ran from the Engenho do Meio to the Engenho de Cima after work on Saturday night just as he did several times a week. I had a basin of hot water ready for him to take his bath.

Josef took the part of my father and Olukoya spoke for Tomba. Josef poured libation, speaking to my ancestors, first in my own language, of which, at his insistence, I had taught him a few words, and then in Fante. Olukoya did the same, speaking in Portuguese so that all could understand. Josef called on the ancestors to bless the union of their daughter (that is, me) with the man I had chosen to be the father of my children. Olukoya had a more difficult task. He and Tomba had become close friends. Tomba had told him about his unusual childhood and about his ignorance as to who his forebears were. He had been brought up without any system of belief and religion played no part in his life. He had no family apart from Ibrahima, who might or might not have been his father, and therefore recognized no ancestors. So Olukoya addressed his words to the ancestors of all the African slaves. He spoke of Tomba's struggle against the slave trade in his part of Africa and of his attempt, with me, to take control of *The Love of Liberty*. He spoke of his courage and he called on the ancestors to watch over him and his new family, not as a man of this or that nation, but as an African.

We passed a bowl of cachaça round and each of us drank from it. Then the older women and those who had feigned illness so that they could spend the day cooking, brought in the wedding meal, which they had improvised from bush meat trapped in the forest, a stolen sheep, and the produce of our allotments.

Drums were beaten and we sang and danced around the fire.

Old Benedito came to us after Mass the following day and advised us both, for the sake of our eternal souls, to beg the priest to marry us in church. We promised to consider his advice. I asked the Senhora, who had returned to the Engenho de Cima after Miranda's marriage, to speak to the Senhor on my behalf, but my mistress thought it better that I make my request to the Senhor in person.

The Senhor was playing chess with Father Isaac on the veranda.

"Senhor, Father, I beg permission to make a request," I told them.

"What is it?" grunted the Senhor.

"I want to get married, Senhor."

"Who is the man?" asked the priest.

"His name is João, Father."

"I have no slave of that name," said the Senhor.

"He belongs to the Engenho do Meio, Senhor."

"Out of the question," replied the Senhor. "Find yourself a man in this engenho."

He turned to the priest. "I won't have my slaves marrying outsiders, Father," he said. "It only causes trouble."

"Senhor, I beg you. Would the Senhor not consider buying João from the senhor at the Engenho do Meio; or selling me to the senhor there?"

"I will think about it. Now, clear these things away."

"I don't mind what the Church says," I heard him say as I went through the door, "marriage is not a proper institution for slaves."

I paused to hear the rest.

"When they get tired of their spouses, they have a tendency to poison them. Then the poor owner loses a slave through no fault of his own. What do you think, Father?"

"That is certainly a risk, Senhor. I have heard of such cases. The Church, need I say it, is in favor of marriage in principle. In practice, the problem is that Africans are so lascivious that, once they are married, they regularly practice adultery; and that is an affront to the Church."

I was busy preparing their bedroom for Senhor and Senhora Williams when Miranda walked in. Her face lit up when she saw me.

"Ama, *awâwâwâ*," she said as we approached, using the Asante which I had taught her.

"Senhora Miranda, *atúù*," I replied as we embraced.

We stepped back and held each other at arm's length. Each of us looked at the other; then, eyes wide, each pointed at the other's belly and we giggled. We embraced again. Then we went to sit side by side on the bed.

"Tell me all the news," Miranda demanded. "I want to know exactly what has happened here since I left. My mother tells me nothing; well, nothing of any importance. I didn't even suspect that you were pregnant, let alone married. All of a sudden. Who is he?"

"He is called João. He comes from the Engenho do Meio. But we are not married. Not in church, anyway. The Senhor would not permit it."

I gave Tomba the name by which the Portuguese knew him.

"What nonsense, Ama," Miranda said.

I knew the look of concern on her face was genuine.

"Why, in heaven's name?"

Marriage to Williams, or was it living in Salvador, had changed Miranda. Such a casual profanity would never have passed her lips when she was a child.

"I think it would be better if you asked the Senhor that question yourself, Senhora Miranda," I replied, "but it is not really important. Everyone knows we are married. But tell me about yourself. How long are you going to stay?"

"Until my baby is born. Senhor Gavin says he needs a break from my extravagant habits. He complains that I am driving him into debt. So my pregnancy has provided him with a convenient excuse to send me home to Mother. For the duration, at least."

"Won't you miss him?"

"Of course, but he has promised to come down at least twice a month. He says he is going to get Josef to teach him how to sail. Oh, Ama. He is such a wonderful husband. Not at all like the stuffy Portuguese men. He has taught me so much. Do you know that I can read and write English now? And speak it a little, too."

"I don't believe you. Show me."

"Heh! Cheeky, cheeky! Speaking to your mistress like that. I'll have to report you to the Senhor."

She saw me start at the rebuke, smiled at her little joke, and kissed me on the cheek.

"Tchtt! Tchtt! You didn't take me seriously, did you? You see, my little one-eyed beauty, I have penetrated your disguise. I know all your secrets. Senhor Gavin has told me everything about you. Everything!"

"Everything?"

"Everything! You wicked girl. Why did you keep so many secrets from me? Don't you see? Now we can talk away in English and, when Senhor Gavin is not around, no one else will be able to understand a word."

"I don't think the Senhora would approve of that. Do you?"

"Hmm! Perhaps you are right. I didn't think of that. But at least we can read to each other. Story books. Novels. I love English novels, don't you? They are so much more interesting than those boring Portuguese stories about the saints. Realistic, Senhor Gavin says."

"What have you been reading?"

"*Tom Jones*. *Tom Jones* is my favorite. And *Pamela*. She is so brave. Heh! Senhor Gavin says that when he knew you before, your name was Pamela. Is that true? How many other names do you have, dear Ama, which you have never told me about? You really are a most secretive person. I want you to vow to me that from now on you will have no secrets from me, not a single one. And I will make the same vow to you. Ama, promise!"

"Senhorita Miranda, I mean Senhora, how you have changed! The ideas that just come tumbling out, one after the other!"

"Ama, your vow! Repeat after me, 'I vow that I will never

keep another secret from Miranda, so help me God,' and cross your heart."

"Senhora, I cannot do that."

"Why not? Why not? Ama, you are not my real friend. I would do anything for you, anything. And when I ask you for just this small favor, you refuse. I think I am going to cry."

I put my arm around her shoulder and hugged her. Miranda sank her head into my breast. I rubbed her back, comforting her as I had done when she was just a girl, before she had married. After a moment, she sat up straight.

"I've changed my mind," she said. "I don't think I shall cry. But tell me why you won't take my vow, you little vixen."

"I beg your pardon, Senhora, I am not your little vixen; nor anyone else's for that matter," I said.

It struck me that Miranda was acting out the part of a romantic heroine in one of the novels her husband had given her to read. I smiled, recalling the idle months I had spent reading my way through Mijn Heer's library. Then a thought struck me.

"Tell me, tell me," insisted Miranda.

"In a moment," I replied. "But first I want to ask you something. Those books which Senhor Gavin has been giving you to read, are they brand new, or do they have someone else's name written inside the front cover?"

"How did you know that? My mother always said she suspected you of being a witch. Have you been practicing black magic with your drums, and cutting the throats of poor cockerels and things?"

"What was the name?"

"I forget. I've never seen a name like that before. It's not Portuguese and not English."

"Try to remember."

Miranda smiled slyly.

"You tell me," she suggested. "Guess the name and I'll tell you if you're right."

"Pieter de Bruyn," I said.

Miranda looked at me, flabbergasted.

"My mother was right," she said. "You are a witch. How could you possibly know that?"

"Now, your vow," I said, quickly changing the subject. "Are you going to tell me all the intimate secrets which you and Senhor Gavin share? How would he feel about that?"

Miranda put her hand over her mouth and stared at me.

"I didn't think about that," she said, and then, almost at once, her face brightened and she continued with a note of triumph in her voice.

"It's simple," she said. "We can leave those out. 'All secrets except those shared with husbands.'"

"You win that one," I said. "By the way, has Senhor Gavin taught you to play chess?"

"Yes, but I'm not very good at it. It's so boring."

"Let's make it more interesting. I challenge you to a game.

Only this time, the rules will be different. I shall play with the white pieces, but only eight of them: the king and the queen, the knights, the bishops, and the rooks; no pawns. You'll play black and you will also have eight pieces, only they will all be pawns. What's more, when it is my turn to move, you must warn me in advance just what move you plan to make next. Oh, yes, and since I'm playing white, I'll make the first move."

Miranda looked puzzled.

"Ama, I don't understand you. That wouldn't be fair. I wouldn't have a chance."

I took her hands.

"Senhora Miranda, it's a sort of parable, like those in the Bible."

Miranda looked at me, a puzzled expression on her face.

"Senhor Gavin told me how you lost your eye," she said. "No, I give up. I never was much good at riddles. Explain it to me."

"It's simple, Senhora," I said. "The white queen is ... you; and the black pawns are us, your Africans. And you are asking us to tell you all our secrets. You see, Senhora Miranda, you are the daughter of the Senhor. I am his slave; I am your slave. I love you dearly and I know that you love me, too, but I am still your slave. Can't we just let each of us decide which of our secrets we want to share?"

Miranda got up and went to the window. She stood there a long time, looking out toward the horses in the paddock.

When she spoke, it was in such a low voice that I had to strain to hear her.

"Senhor Gavin's uncle in London sent him a new book recently. Senhor Gavin says he can't put it down, but that I would find it boring, so he just tells me what it says. He is so clever, Senhor Gavin. Sometimes I wish I were a man."

She came back and sat on the floor, legs crossed, in front of me, looking up at me.

"The author, Dr. Adam Smith, says that slavery is stupid and that it is also wicked. He says it spoils the soil. He says it costs us more to keep you all as slaves than it would if we gave you your freedom and paid you a wage, like we do with the overseers and the Tupi. He says the real reason that we keep slaves is not that it makes us rich, but that it makes us feel powerful, especially our men. Senhor Gavin says that the more he thinks about it, the more he sees the truth in Dr. Smith's arguments."

I saw that Miranda was crying. I said nothing but took a handkerchief and wiped the tears from her cheeks.

"Ama," she said, "if one day the Engenho de Cima becomes mine, I will set every slave here free. And you will be the first."

"Hush," I replied. "You must not speak of your parents' death like that. I believe you; from the bottom of my heart, I believe you. But please don't tell the Senhor the way you feel; nor the Senhora. Let it be a secret between us, just the two of us."

Chapter Eleven

Zacharias

"Now Kwame," my mother says to me, "the time has come for you to enter this story. You are a father; and fathers should know something about childbirth. So I am going to tell you about your own birth."

That is not something I want to hear. When our daughter Carlota was born, I found something else to occupy me, far away from Iphigenia. I left everything to the midwives. I don't agree with my mother. Childbirth is the business of women. But she is my mother and I must listen to her and put her story down on paper.

In her account of my birth, she does not mention that I was born out of wedlock. It might have been the old Senhor's fault for refusing to allow my parents to marry in church, but the truth is that they lived in sin throughout their life together. That doesn't seem to concern her. It does concern me.

There is something else which troubles me as much.

"My Mother," I ask her, "is it really true that even before I was born, Senhora Miranda promised to give you your freedom?"

"Yes, it is true," she says.

I don't tell her that Senhora Miranda has made the same promise to me.

"Why hasn't she kept her promise?" I ask.

"That is a question you must direct to Senhora Miranda."

Ama's story

Miranda's child arrived first.

Together, she and I had prepared one of the guest rooms for the delivery. When her waters broke, we sent down to the senzalas for the midwives. The women surrounded her bed, kept her arms and legs moving, and urged her to "push, push, Senhora." Benedito's wife offered her a crucifix to kiss, put a rosary on her belly, and prayed to Santa Miranda to watch over her namesake. The old Senhora, Miranda's mother, walked up and down, giving orders to which the women paid no attention; for once, it was they who were in charge. I sat by her side throughout; it was I who announced to Miranda that her baby was a girl; I who held the child while the cord was cut and smeared with oil and pepper; and I who took it upon myself to give the infant her first bath.

Miranda insisted that when my turn came, a week later,

I should give birth on the same bed in the same room. The scene was much the same, except for the absence of the Senhora, who was not well, and the reversal of our roles. But whereas Miranda's labor had been short, mine was long and painful. The child, as you know, was a boy. Miranda bathed you but by the time she brought you to show to me, so she told me later, I had fallen into an exhausted sleep.

When I woke, it was evening and the candles had been lit. Miranda sat on an upright chair by my side, holding you. You were asleep. Senhor Gavin sat in an armchair nearby.

Tomba stood at the end of the bed. I watched him shift his weight from one bare foot to the other. Senhor Williams had never recognized my João as the Tomba who had been my co-conspirator on board ship, but Tomba was always nervous in his presence, fearing that revelation of the past might result in his being sold to a distant engenho. He was uncomfortable in the presence of all whites, but Williams more so than others. Miranda, too, had failed to win his confidence, though not from want of trying. Tomba had his reservations about my friendly relationship with my mistress, and had tried to persuade me to have my child in our cabin rather than in the *casa grande*; but I had persuaded him, with some difficulty, that it would be in the baby's best interest to accept Miranda's kindness.

Now Miranda lifted you up.

"João, take him and show him to Ama," she commanded.

Tomba did what he was told. We smiled at one another as Miranda brought a candle closer so that I could inspect you.

"Here, João, won't you sit down?" Miranda said, pulling a chair forward for him, but he preferred to remain standing.

I saw Senhor Gavin incline his head in a signal to his wife that they should leave us alone together. Miranda rose and then hesitated.

"Wait," she said. "There is one thing I must discuss with Ama before we go. Senhor Gavin has to return to Salvador soon. We have decided to have our baby baptized in the chapel on Sunday, a week from tomorrow. We are going to call her Elizabeth. If you will agree, I ... we, would like you to have your baby baptized on the same day. We can discuss it later, but I thought you might like to talk about what name you intend to give him while João is here."

She leant down to kiss me on the forehead.

"I'll come back and bring you some soup after João has left," she said.

It was Miranda's suggestion that you be baptized with the name of Zacharias, the father of John the Baptist.

"My brother is going to be Elizabeth's godfather and I have persuaded Senhor Gavin to be godfather to Zacharias, unless you have someone else in mind, that is."

"Senhora Miranda, are you sure there will be no objection?" I asked. "Zacharias and Elizabeth were husband

and wife, you know."

"And that means your Zacharias is going to marry my Elizabeth? What rubbish, Ama. Sometimes I think you are just too sensitive."

By the Sunday of the baptism, we had already given you a name. The day before, the seventh day after your birth, I rose very early, an hour before the work bell was due to sound. Josef went from cabin to cabin in the dark, rousing our friends. When they had assembled at the usual place, he poured libation, praying briefly in Fante and then switching to Portuguese so that all could understand.

"Spirits of our forefathers, we greet you. I am Josef from Anomabu. With me are all the Africans of the Engenho de Cima. Spirits of our forefathers, we bring you this drink and beg you to accept it. We have risen early this morning to welcome a new arrival in our midst."

"Who is the mother of this child?" he asked.

"I, Ama."

"And the father?"

"I, Tomba."

"Ancestors of Ama and of Tomba, bear witness, we beg you, to the arrival of their first child. It is a boy. Watch over him, guard him, make him strong and wise, honest and compassionate."

"Tomba, what name do you give to this child?"

"I call him Kwame for the spirit of the day on which he

was born; and I call him Zumbi in honor of the great King of Palmares."

Everyone clapped their hands. Josef spilled *cachaça* on the ground.

"Spirit of Zumbi of Palmares, we call upon you. Enter into this our boy-child and make him great, even as you are great."

Josef sat down on a stool and I handed you to him.

He dipped his right forefinger into a small bowl of water and used it to wet your lips and tongue. He did the same again, and then a third time. Then he addressed you.

"Kwame Zumbi, if you say this is water, let it be water which I place upon your tongue."

Wono offered him another small bowl, this one containing *cachaça*. He performed the same custom, saying, "Kwame Zumbi, if you say this is *cachaça*, let it be *cachaça* which I place upon your tongue."

Finally he said to you, "Kwame Zumbi, I have shown you the difference between water and strong drink. If you say it is black you see, let it truly be black. If you say it is white you see, let it be white."

He rose and handed you to me. Tomba drank from the bowl of *cachaça* and I also took a sip.

"Now we have shown your son to the ancestors," Josef told us, "you are free to bring him out of doors."

Our friends lined up to shake our hands. Then the work bell rang.

Zacharias

This pagan rite performed upon me as a child has no force, thank the Lord. It is null and void, wiped out, canceled, by my baptism. When I return to Salvador, I shall tell Senhora Miranda how grateful I am to her for insisting that I be baptized. And I may ask her proud daughter, Senhorita Elizabeth, if she knows that the two of us were baptized on the same Sunday, in the same church, with the same holy water. I wonder what she'll say to that. If she denies it, I'll call her mother as my witness.

As for my own mother, when I ask her to tell me about my baptism, she says she can't remember. I fear that she might be beyond salvation. Nevertheless, I shall continue to honor her as the fifth commandment enjoins, and I shall redouble my prayers that she may see the light.

Ama's story

Life at the Engenho de Cima hardly changed. The annual cycle of the *safra*, of St. John's Day and the feasts of the Virgin Mary and the other saints, of Christmas and Easter, continued in an unbroken succession. Slaves worked the ten years, more or less, which fate has allotted to us, died, and were replaced by new ones from Africa. One year slipped into the next.

In spite of their promises, Senhor Gavin and Senhora Miranda seldom visited the Engenho.

Josef brought us news of them. Senhor Gavin's business interests kept him occupied and Senhora Miranda, encouraged by her husband, became increasingly involved in the high society of Salvador. When they did come, they never brought Elizabeth.

The Senhor became increasingly frail, but steadfastly refused to follow his slaves to the grave. The Senhora's hair turned white and she spent more and more of her time in prayer and reading the lives of the saints, leaving the day-to-day running of the *casa grande* to me and the other house slaves. Increasingly Jesus Vasconcellos took over the running of the business, although the Senhor, in spite of his decrepitude, never allowed him an entirely free hand.

Olukoya remained a tower of strength, advising, arbitrating, leading by example. He has always been sustained by an unwavering conviction of the value of what we brought with us from Africa and by a vision of a better future, an African Brazil.

Old Benedito, on the other hand, was confirmed in his faith by the steady growth in the number of converts.

Olukoya was (and still is) intolerant of human failings, particularly those that cause pain to others; in the other camp, Father Isaac, behind the curtain of the confessional, casually dispensed total absolution from the most abominable behavior at the price of a few Hail Mary's and the admonition to go and sin no more. Some of us kept a foot in both camps; but to me that was sheer hypocrisy.

The Senhor could no longer walk from his bedroom to his rocking chair on the veranda. Bernardo and Tomás, the Hausa blacksmith, fashioned a simple wheelchair for him. Then he became too weak to sit up and had to lie all day and night in his darkened bedroom. I fed him, washed him, changed his bedclothes, and treated his sores as best I could. He was heavy, and turning him several times a day strained my back. It still troubles me. The Senhora visited him once a day, prayed, and then left him to our tender mercies. Father Isaac said a perfunctory Mass in his bedroom once a week. Then the Senhor became incontinent. I wiped him and washed him and dried him; but try as I might, I could not clear the pervasive smell of excrement from his room. The Senhora stopped coming to pray by his side. I sat down at his desk, found quill and ink, and wrote to Miranda. Josef took the letter to Salvador. Miranda sent her reply by word of mouth: she had one or two urgent matters to attend to; she would come as soon as she had dealt with them.

The Senhor was dying. He had not eaten for several days and his breathing was irregular. I called the priest. Father Isaac administered the extreme unction, fanning his own face while he did so in an attempt to dissipate the foul smell of illness and death. A pale wraith appeared at the door but did not come in; it was the Senhora. I was alone with the old man when he died.

"Senhora," I told her, "the Senhor is dead."

She did not seem to hear, so I repeated the words loudly in her ear.

"I heard you. I may be old but I'm not deaf," she replied and crossed herself three times.

The priest, on hearing the news, made the same sign.

I went down to the carpentry shop.

"Bernardo," I told the carpenter in Fante, "dust off his coffin and send it up. I'm worn out. I'm going to tell Josef to take the news to Salvador and then I'm going to sleep. I'll wash his body when I wake up."

Zacharias

"My Mother," I tell her, "you may not be a Christian, but that was Christian work you did, succoring the sick and dying."

"Thank you, Kwame," she says.

She still insists on calling me Kwame.

"Thank you," she says. "I never did hear those two words pass the old Senhor's lips. He had little love for me. And his family hardly showed any gratitude for the way I nursed him in his last days. Sometimes I think I should have just let him rot in his own excrement."

It is sad. She is my mother and has many fine qualities, but I have to say it: she lacks the capacity for forgiveness.

Ama's story

By the time Miranda and her brothers arrived, everything was ready; the grave was dug; I had dressed the Senhor's shrunken body in the uniform of a colonel of the militia, which I found in his trunk; the coffin had been placed on the veranda under an awning to keep off the sun; the kitchen staff had made their preparations to cope with the mourners expected from the surrounding districts.

Miranda lifted her veil and kissed me on both cheeks.

"You don't know how grateful I am for all you have done," she told me.

Senhor Gavin nodded.

"Elizabeth, dear," said Miranda, "this is Ama. Remember I told you her son is just a week younger than you are? Ama where is Zacharias? I would love to see him."

Elizabeth was dressed in black, a miniature copy of her elegant mother. I knelt down and took her hands.

"Elizabeth, let me look at you. You are so pretty. How old are you now?"

But she ignored me.

"Mama," she said, "I want to see the horses and the sheep and the pigs."

Zacharias

Yes, Elizabeth, Senhorita Elizabeth Williams, Miss High-and-Mighty, Nose-in-the-Air. Judging by what my mother says, she must have been born with those airs. Thank the Lord I am not like that.

When I first arrived in Salvador with Senhora Miranda, Elizabeth welcomed me. She was stuck all alone in that big house, except when daughters of the Senhora's friends came to visit. When there were just the two of us together, she didn't mind playing with me. What choice did she have? But when her friends came, she let me know I was her slave. I used to hide. For one thing, I didn't want to play with girls but, more important, I didn't want to be humiliated by them. If Senhora Miranda had known how her daughter treated me when she wasn't around, she would have reprimanded her; but once we had finished our lessons, we didn't see much of the Senhora.

My mother asks me, "How is Elizabeth? She must surely be married by now? Does she have children?"

"My mother," I tell her, "Elizabeth is still Senhorita Elizabeth. None of the Portuguese boys are good enough for her. She quotes a proverb that says that a really virtuous Portuguese woman leaves her home only three times during her lifetime, once for her christening, once for her marriage, and once for her funeral. She says she refuses to be that virtuous Portuguese woman. She wants the Senhor and the Senhora to take her to London to find an English husband."

Ama's story

The family met to read the old Senhor's will.

Old Benedito was given his freedom. But old Benedito was already dead.

The Senhor's property was to pass to the Senhora. The children would inherit their shares only after their mother's death. The Senhora crossed herself and took no further part in the proceedings. It was decided that the eldest son would administer the Engenho, but since he was running his own sugar plantation, they had to appoint a manager. Jesus Vasconcellos was the obvious choice.

The Senhora went to live in Salvador. Father Isaac went there, too.

"Ama, come with me to Salvador," Miranda said.

"What about my son, Senhora? And João?" I asked.

"Of course, you would bring Zacharias. But João doesn't belong to us. I would have to talk to Senhor Gavin about him."

Senhor Gavin made an offer to Tomba's master at the Engenho do Meio, but the senhor refused to sell. Tomba was a key man in the running of his mill. So, with Senhora Miranda's reluctant consent, we stayed put.

Chapter Twelve

Ama's story

The next year, you turned ten. Vasconcellos ordered you to join one of the field gangs.

One day you returned after dark, as usual, so exhausted that you would have fallen asleep without eating if I had not forced you to stay awake. I had stopped delivering the produce of my allotment to the casa grande; the money was too small and there was always an argument about payment. Our meat allocation was so worm-ridden that I refused to use it; and Vasconcellos never let go of the keys to the kitchen store.

Tomba brought us whatever he could spare from his own rations. It was this and the yield of his Sunday trapping and fishing that kept us going.

I watched over you as you fell asleep. I covered you and rose to return to the *casa grande* to serve Senhor Jesus his evening meal.

As I was leaving the cabin, head bowed, worrying about your future, I heard the cry, "Fire, fire."

Looking up, I saw a red glow in the sky above the cane fields. Then the work bell rang—the slaves were being summoned to fight the inferno. Undecided as to what to do, I went back into the cabin and looked at your sleeping form. It would be at least an hour before Tomba arrived.

"Kwame, wake up!" I said.

You resisted, pulling the blanket back over your head. I grabbed you under the armpits and pulled you to your feet.

"Mama, what is it?" you asked.

"Here, take your blanket. You are going to sleep in the cave tonight."

There is a small crevice in the rocks on the hillside where, in earlier days, I would go to read. You still loved to hide in it: it was your secret refuge, the only place you could call your own. I pushed you before me, threading a way past the field slaves as they came stumbling out of their cabins in the dark.

Zacharias

I started work when I was just ten? Why don't I remember? But the cave—I seem to remember a cave. Not really a cave, just a small opening in the rocks with room for two or three small children to hide.

"My Mother," I ask, "is that cave still there?"

"Of course," she replies. "Where do you think it might have moved, to Salvador?"

That is my mother's sort of joke.

"We passed it on our way to the allotment last Sunday. Remind me next time and I'll point it out to you."

How will you do that, I wonder, if you can't see; but I keep my silence.

Ama's story

Maria Cabinda, the cook, was standing at the kitchen door, looking out at the glow in the dark sky.

She was worried about her husband, who would be fighting the fire, and about her two young children. If the wind were to turn, the fire might cut the men off from the stream. Then they would be unable to stop the inferno sweeping in from the fields, through to the yard and the mill, and on to the *senzalas*.

"Go and bring them up here," I suggested, but Maria was afraid of Senhor Jesus's wrath. She had done that once before when one of them had had a high fever. Finding them asleep in a corner of the kitchen had driven him into a frenzy of rage.

I told her what I had done with you. Maria knew where the cave was.

"If you like, take them there and let them sleep with Kwame. When Tomba comes, I'll ask him to go up and spend the night with them. Don't worry, I'll cover for you. I'll tell Jesus you have gone to help fight the fire. He could hardly complain about that. And I'll finish the cooking."

The fire turned out to be less serious than the height of the flames had suggested. Only three fields were burnt.

Vasconcellos trudged up to the *casa grande,* his face streaked with ash. I turned my head to hide my grin.

"Rum!" he commanded.

He didn't even notice the absence of the cook. I served him his food. By the time he had finished the second course, the bottle was half empty. He started to mumble to himself. Returning from the kitchen with the third course, I saw him bang the heavy table with his fist. He turned and glared at me. I lowered my eye.

When he had finished eating, I cleared the table. Then I went back to the dining room. He was still sitting there, staring at the empty bottle.

"Will there be anything else, Senhor?" I asked quietly.

He turned to stare at me. Then he drained the dregs of the rum from his glass.

"Will there be anything else, Senhor?" he mimicked. "Yes, One-eye, there will be something else."

He rose and grabbed me at once by the shoulders, pulling me toward him. I struggled to free myself but he was too strong. He forced my lips apart and drove his tongue into my mouth. I tasted the foulness and the rum. Almost instinctively, I sank my teeth into his lower lip. He screamed in agony and pushed me so violently that I fell backwards. My head struck the stone floor. I lay there, stunned. He dropped onto me and ripped my cloth off. Then he was inside me, thrusting away his hatred and frustration.

When he had finished with me, he stood over me where I lay sobbing on the floor. He said nothing. I turned over on my side, hiding my face in my hands. Then (I am using my imagination because I didn't see this, only felt the result) he drew his right boot back and deliberately, with all his strength, kicked me.

When I came to, he had gone. Slowly, painfully, I got to my knees. Taking hold of the edge of the table, I pulled myself to my feet. I stood still for a while, dizzy, afraid that I would faint again. Then, step by step, I crossed the open space to the nearest wall. I closed my eye and rested my weight against the door post. Step by step again, across the kitchen. I went out and, by force of long habit, took the key and locked the door. I met no one as I limped and stumbled to the *senzalas*. All was quiet; the exhausted fire fighters had trudged back to their hovels and quickly fallen asleep.

Tomba came out of the cabin. He had just arrived. The moon had risen. I could see the sweat glistening on his bare torso.

"Ama," he asked as he saw me approaching, "where's Kwame?"

Then he saw that something was amiss.

"Ama, what's wrong?" he asked as he came to help me.

"Senhor Jesus," I replied. "He raped me."

"Vasconcellos raped you?"

Rape happened so regularly, we women almost accepted it as part of the condition of our lives. But it had never before happened to Tomba's Ama.

"Tomba," I asked him wearily, "bring me water, I beg you."

He ministered to my needs, wiped my face, blew up the embers of the fire and put a basin of water on it. I told him about the burning cane fields and what I had done with Kwame. Then I stretched out to try to sleep.

"Have you got a knife?" he asked me.

"Not here," I replied without opening my eye. "In the kitchen."

"Where's the key?" he asked.

I sat up.

"No, Tomba, no!"

"Where's the key?" he demanded.

I felt the corner of my cloth.

"I don't have it. I must have left it in the door or dropped it on the way. Tomba, don't do it. I beg you, Tomba. I beg you."

I was sobbing now.

"Can you walk?" he asked me, gently but firmly forcing me to my feet.

"Tomba, what will you achieve? You will bring tragedy down on all our heads. Think of Kwame. Let it be. You cannot reverse what has been done."

"Come," he told me. "I might need your help."

Zacharias

My Mother, My Mother. What you have been through in your life.

"My Mother," I say, "I am so sorry."

"It was a long time ago," she says, "and Jesus Vasconcellos was punished for what he did to me."

"By my father?" I ask.

"By your father," she replies.

I fear what is to come.

"My Mother," I say, "this has been a long session. I can see that you are exhausted. Let us leave it until tomorrow."

"No," she says, "I must finish this part of the story now. If I don't, I shall not be able to sleep tonight.

"How much paper do you have left?" she asks.

Ama's story

We didn't find the key and it wasn't in the kitchen door. Tomba whispered instructions to me.

"For the last time, Tomba, I beg you. Remember what we did together on the ship."

"It is because of that, that I must do this," he said. "Now, are you ready? Do what I say."

He banged on the jalousie shutters of Jesus's bedroom. At first there was no answer and I hoped against hope that in his drunken state, the man had fallen asleep somewhere out of earshot. But then we heard his half-awake, slurred speech.

"Who the hell is that making that confounded row?"

"Senhor Jesus. It is I, Ama, One-eye."

"Go away. I'll have you whipped to an inch of your life in the morning if you don't stop that row."

"Senhor. The fire has started again. They have set the cane fields on fire."

That woke him up, drunk as he was. We heard him swear as he struggled to pull on his boots. We went round to the veranda. I stood a little way off, where he would see me in the moonlight as he opened the door. We heard him fumble with the key. The door opened and he stepped out. He was holding a musket at waist height, a finger on the trigger. Tomba, standing beside the door, felled him with a single blow.

In a moment Tomba had dragged him back into the house.

"Ama, come quickly. Bring the gun and close the door behind you. Now lock it. Do you have a candle? And some rope to tie him with?"

He had already stuffed a cloth into the man's mouth. Now he wound it round and round his head to secure the gag. Then he turned him face down and sat on him.

I returned, not with a rope but with a pair of manacles and a pair of leg-irons.

"The keys are in the locks," I told him.

"Excellent," he replied. "Now a knife, the sharpest you can find."

"Tomba, I beg you. It is enough. They will torture you before they kill you."

"Never mind. Do as I say."

"What about Kwame? And me?"

"I must do what I must do."

In the kitchen I sat down, sank my head upon the table, and tried to consider my options. I could run to Olukoya and Josef for help. But by the time they arrived, Tomba would already have found a weapon and done his worst. Then I would have to live out my years with the knowledge that I had failed him. And what could Olukoya and Josef do but give him up to the militia?

"Well?"

Tomba was standing in the doorway. I pointed to the drawer where the knives were kept. He turned the contents out onto the table.

"Tomba, for the last time."

I put my arm on his naked back and caressed him. He shook me off and continued to examine each of the knives in turn.

I went to the doorway and lay down on the floor, face down, with my head toward him.

"What are you doing?" he asked.

"I am prostrating myself before you, as the Yorubas do

before their gods. Kill me, rather."

He stepped over me. I rose and followed him.

He turned the man over and sat down on his stomach. Jesus's manacled hands were behind his back, under him. Tomba put the instruments down beside him. Then he removed the gag.

"You may say your last prayers," he told the manager of the Engenho de Cima.

"Who are you?" Vasconcellos demanded. "I warn you. Release me at once or it will go hard with you."

"It will go hard with me anyway, shit-face. Make your confession and beg for absolution before I cut out your tongue."

I was shocked. I had never heard Tomba use foul language before. I hugged myself and rocked from foot to foot. Closing my eye, I tried to summon up a vision of Itsho. But all I could see was a dark void.

"Right, Senhor Jesus," said Tomba, "you've had your chance. No prayers."

He forced the man's mouth open and wedged a wooden spoon between his teeth. Then he seized Vasconcellos's tongue with a pair of tongs and pulled it out of his mouth and sliced it off. Blood spurted over him. As he rose to his feet, I caught a glimpse of the terror in his victim's eyes. Then I threw up.

When I rose to my feet, Tomba had pulled the man's pants

down. Now he ripped off his blood-soaked shirt as well. The manager lay naked. Tomba took a cushion from a chair and put it under the man's head.

"I want you to have a good view of this," he told Vasconcellos.

Using his knees, he forced the man's legs apart. He waved the blood-stained knife before the man's eyes.

"Tomba, no, no!"

I tried to pull him away but he shrugged me off. I ran to the door, turned the key, and in a moment was running down to the senzalas.

Zacharias

I lie awake, listening to my mother's regular breathing.

The picture of the terrible punishment which my father inflicted on the Portuguese man will not leave my mind. My father had no right to do what he did. He should have left the rapist to the judgment of God. I fear that he must be burning in the eternal flames of hell.

My mother has been carrying this burden of memory all these years. Now, with its telling, she is at peace. I can hear it from her relaxed breathing. She has passed the burden on to me. I must bear it now. For her, "it was a long time ago," but for me, it is as if it happened today.

Kneeling, I pray, "Dear God, my father acted in passion. Please forgive him, please forgive him."

CHAPTER THIRTEEN

Ama

Tabitsha my mother is here, and Itsho, and Tomba.

"Tomba," I say, "I have told him. I have told Kwame the whole story. All that remains is the difficult task of telling him how you died, but I will manage that. Tomorrow I will tell him that. And then it will be finished and I can rest."

They all nod. They have heard me but they say nothing.

Suddenly, out of a clear sky, lightning strikes. It strikes me.

"Kwame, Kwame," I call out.

"My Mother, what is it?" I hear his reply.

The pain in my head is unbearable; it is as if the lightning has ripped my skull apart. I try to sit up but I cannot move. My right side is without feeling. I am dying. Death waited until I had finished my story. Now he has come for me. Soon it will be all over. I cry out for Tabitsha my mother, and Itsho, and Tomba, but they are no longer there. At least the pain is less. I am falling, falling ...

Zacharias

Our sleeping mats are stretched out side by side on the floor of my mother's cabin. I lie on my back, unable to sleep, listening to her steady breathing and turning her terrible story over in my mind.

Suddenly she cries out.

"Kwame, Kwame," she calls.

"My Mother, what is it?" I ask, but there is no answer.

It is dark inside my mother's cabin. I open the door to let in some light and then I go to her. At first I fear that she is dead, but I can hear her breathing, fitful, no longer regular as it was before. I panic. I need help. I run to Josef and Wono's cabin. Wono says Josef arrived from Salvador after dark. He was tired and has just fallen asleep. She wakes him and he follows us with an oil lamp.

"My Mother, can you hear me?" I ask, but again there is no response.

"I think it is a stroke," I say. "The old Senhora had a stroke. She could not move her arm and her leg on her right side and when she spoke, it was impossible to understand what she was trying to say. She lived like that for a year before she died. Josef, do you remember?"

"Wono, what shall we do?" Josef asks.

"Let us lift her onto the bed," Wono says. "Then bring

my mat. I will keep watch. There is nothing we can do until morning."

I go with Josef.

"Kwame, I am sorry," he says. "This has happened at the wrong time."

Any time to have a stroke is the wrong time, I think.

"What do you mean?" I ask.

"I brought a message from Salvador. You are to return at once. I am to take you first thing in the morning."

"Why?" I ask.

He looks at me. Then he covers his face with the palms of his hands. He stands like that, silent, for a few moments. He looks exhausted.

"I'll tell you later," he says, dropping his hands. "Here, take Wono's mat. Go and be with your mother. I must get some sleep."

The sky is blue, the sea calm, the sun not yet as hot as it will be later in the day. A light breeze fills our sail, propelling us across the Bay of All the Saints to Salvador. Josef has put me in control of the rudder.

He says, "What could Senhor Fonseca do, after all? He takes his orders from Senhor Gavin. You must ask Senhora Miranda to let you come straight back with me. In the meantime, Wono and Ayo will take good care of your mother. She seemed to be a little better this morning. What do you think?"

I don't really believe it but I nod all the same.

"Did she finish telling you her story?" he asks, tapping the leather bag which he uses to keep the letters dry, the letters he carries between Salvador and the Engenho. My mother's manuscript is in that satchel.

"Almost," I reply. "She told me what my father did ..."

"Ah, Senhor Jesus," says Josef. "He got what he deserved." He pauses as he pulls the sail around to make a change in course. "Do you want to hear the end of the story?" he asks.

Fearing more unpleasant surprises, I pause before I nod and mouth my silent consent.

"Ama called us, Olukoya, Wono, and me. When we got to the *casa grande*, Vasconcellos was dead. Your father was sitting on the floor, his back to the wall, covered in blood, the blood of Senhor Jesus.

"It was already midnight. We met in the kitchen and quickly decided to leave the Engenho and head for the forest. Olukoya got us organized. By dawn we were well on our way. The few who refused to join us, we tied them up to clear them of guilt.

"For a few days we lived in freedom. Then our food stocks began to run low. I volunteered to lead a night raid. Foolishly I agreed to let an overseer called Pedro join us. The man was addicted to *cachaça* and when we arrived at the Engenho, his thirst got the better of him and he defected. We knew that the militia would be on its way in the morning, with Pedro as its guide. We knew also, only too well, that we would have no chance against them. Your father volunteered to go and give himself up. He knew that they would execute him but he hoped that Senhor Gavin and Senhora Miranda would have arrived from Salvador and that his surrender might persuade them to spare the rest of us. Your mother insisted on going with him and, of course, they took you along. Do you remember any of this?"

I'm not sure what to say. The truth is that I don't know whether I remember or not. The past is like the dense, early morning fog which sometimes rolls off the sea into the *cidade baixa*.

"There is little more to tell. They set up a court, tried your father, found him guilty of murdering Jesus Vasconcellos, and sentenced him to death by hanging. Your mother told Senhora Miranda how the man had raped her and she begged for mercy, all in vain. The Senhora said it was enough that the rest of us had escaped severe punishment. The truth is that Tomba was not Senhora Miranda's property and his death was no loss to her. And then there were the demands of the militia. Justice! The blacks must be taught a lesson. Mercy? Never! The blacks must be taught a lesson.

"They hanged your father from the branch of a tree. There is more, but I am not sure that I should tell you."

The wind is rising and Josef has to reef the sail.

"Tell me," I insist.

"They wouldn't let us take his body down. It hung there for five days, decomposing. That was to teach us obedience."

"I remember nothing. Where was I all this time?"

"Senhora Miranda took you from your mother and kept you isolated. She wouldn't even let her say goodbye to you before she took you away to Salvador."

A picture comes into my mind. A horse-drawn carriage. I shut my eyes and try to concentrate. It was the first time I had been in one, all red leather and shiny brass. I was so excited.

"Did they take me in a carriage?" I ask.

"Kwame, your memory is coming back. Yes, a carriage with four horses."

I am sitting in the carriage on the leather seat, by a curtained window. I hear the horses neigh. We start moving. I draw the curtain aside. There, hanging from the branch of a tree, is the corpse of a man. The Senhora, sitting beside me, sees it, too. She slaps my hand down and the curtain falls back to hide the vision. She grabs me and forces me across to the other side of her, between her and Senhor Gavin.

I summon up my courage.

"Senhora?"

"Yes, Zacharias."

Her tone discourages enquiry.

"Senhora, I saw ... Was that ...?"

"Zacharias, you saw nothing. Nothing! Do you understand? Nothing! Now what did you see?"

"Senhora. I saw ... nothing."

"That's a good boy. Now just settle down and enjoy the ride."

Josef

The trip across the bay is uneventful. Kwame is deep in thought. From time to time he shakes his head as if in silent conversation with himself. He seems close to tears, but I judge it better to say nothing.

The gateman at the Consulate tells me to report to Senhor Gavin at once. I knock and he calls out to me to enter. He is sitting behind his desk. I greet him and take the papers out of the satchel. I separate the letters from the Engenho and hand them to him. When I start to replace Ama's manuscript, the Senhor asks, "What's that?"

"Oh, it's nothing," I tell him, with a bad feeling in the pit of my stomach.

"Nothing?"

"Just some papers Zacharias gave me. I put them in the satchel to keep them dry during the journey.

"Give that to me," he says.

He puts on his spectacles and starts to read.

I stand there, waiting, gently rubbing the carpet with my toes.

"Call Zacharias," he says, without looking up.

When we get back, Ama's manuscript is lying on his desk.

"Zacharias," he says. "Pull up a chair and sit down."

I withdraw and wait, ready to receive his instructions.

"How was your holiday? How is your mother?" he asks Kwame and goes on without waiting for an answer. "Do you want to know why I told Josef to bring you back from the Engenho?"

He picks up the manuscript and puts it down again.

"We are leaving," he says. "For London. Me, the Senhora, and Elizabeth. Tonight we shall sleep on board *The Love of Liberty*. We sail at dawn when the tide turns. Any questions?"

Kwame knows all this. I have told him already. If he has prepared any questions, he decides not to put them. He just looks at his feet.

"The new Consul, Mr. Bates, arrived two days ago on our ship. I will introduce you to him later. From now on, you will report to him."

The other door opens and Senhora Miranda bursts into the room.

"My dear ..." she says (she always calls him that). "Oh, Zacharias, I didn't know you'd arrived. How did you find your mother?"

"I've finished with him, dear," says Senhor Gavin. "You may take him to your office."

"Oh, one thing more, Zacharias," says Senhor Gavin,

taking the manuscript in his hand. "What's this?"

"It is a document, Senhor," Kwame replies, "dictated to me by my mother and given to me by her. It is mine."

"Zacharias, my boy, you forget your status. A slave has no right to own property of any sort without the express permission of his master."

"Oh, Gavin," says the Senhora, "is that really necessary? Come, Zacharias."

Zacharias

Senhora Miranda asks me to sit down. I haven't yet had a chance to greet Iphigenia, my wife, and Nandzi Ama, my daughter. My heart aches for them.

"Zacharias," the Senhora says, "tell me all the news. How is your mother, how is my dear Ama? I really would have loved to give her a hug before we leave for England. Senhor Gavin has told you about our departure? It is your friend Elizabeth. She has no time for the Portuguese boys. If we don't find a husband for her soon, she will turn out to be an old maid."

I wait patiently for the gush of words to end.

"Senhora, last night my mother had a stroke. She cannot move and she has lost the power of speech."

"Oh, my God," says the Senhora and hides her face in her hands.

"Why did you come back to Salvador? Why did you leave her?" she asks.

"The Senhor ordered Josef to bring me back, at all costs," I tell her.

"Of course," she says.

We sit in silence.

"You should go back as soon as possible," she says. "I'll ask Senhor Gavin to speak to the new Consul about it."

Then she asks me, "What was that business with the Senhor?"

I pause, wondering how to reply.

"About some papers?" she says.

"Senhora, my mother dictated the story of her life to me. She intended me to keep the manuscript and to hand it on one day to my daughter. I gave it to Josef to keep in his letter satchel. I guess that Senhor Gavin saw it and took it from him before he had a chance to return it to me."

The door opens. It is Senhor Gavin. He stands at the threshold without entering. He is holding my mother's manuscript.

"Zacharias," he says, shaking it up and down, "I have glanced through this. Very interesting. In fact, unique. I've never seen anything like it before. I shall take it to London and have it published. Your mother will be famous."

That is all. He closes the door behind him.

"Senhora Miranda," I say. "That was not my mother's intention and it is not my wish."

"Oh, don't be difficult, Zacharias. Trust the Senhor. He

knows what he is doing, and you can be assured that he will always act in your best interest. Now, my boy, I will miss you. Have you seen Elizabeth? You must say goodbye to her before we leave."

"Senhora, my mother told me that you promised her many years ago that once the Engenho passed into your hands, you would give her her freedom."

"She told you that, did she? I really don't remember. But what good would it have done her? We have looked after her since she became blind, and we shall continue to do so now that she has had a stroke. If she were free, who would be responsible? Who would house her and feed her and clothe her? Zacharias, I know that slavery is an evil system, in principle at least, but you must be practical."

"Senhora, on several occasions you have promised me my manumission papers. I hope that you have not forgotten."

"Zacharias, I spoke to Senhor Gavin about it just this last week. He says he is sorry but it is just not possible at this time. You are a key man in the Consulate. The new Consul knows little Portuguese. He will depend on your help. Senhor Gavin has promised me that you will get an increase in your wages. If you save wisely, in a few years you will be able to buy your freedom, whether the Senhor approves or not. I am sorry. I hope you understand."

I do understand. Promises mean nothing to these people. I understand that now.

"Senhora, there is one other matter I should like to clear up before you leave. It is about my father, Tomba."

I see a cloud pass over her face.

"What about him?"

"The manager, Jesus Vasconcellos, raped my mother."

"I didn't know that."

"My mother says she told you. It was his custom, raping the slave women."

"I didn't know that."

"My father punished Jesus Vasconcellos for raping my mother. He cut off his tongue to punish him for all the abuse that had issued from his mouth; and then he cut off his genitals to punish him for all the pain and humiliation he had inflicted on my mother and the other women."

She bows her head. I wonder whether she might call Senhor Gavin. She looks up.

"Zacharias, what is this all about? I took you away from the scene of those dreadful events. I have treated you as if you were my own son, Elizabeth's brother. Tell me the truth, have I treated you badly? Have you been short of food, clothing, loving care, even? Have I not taught you to read and write both Portuguese and English, as well as, even better than my own daughter? Now, let's hear no more of this, please. All this happened years ago. It is past history, long past, better forgotten."

"Senhora Miranda, all those years ago when you took

the small boy, which was me, away from my mother, away from the Engenho, do you remember that I pulled aside the curtain of the coach window and saw my father's body hanging from the branch of a tree? You slapped my hand to let the curtain fall back, and you pulled me away from the window and made me repeat: I saw nothing, I saw nothing, I saw nothing. Do you remember? My mother did not tell me this. How could she? Only you and Senhor Gavin and I were there, behind the curtains of that carriage. Do you remember? All these years, I have buried that memory and acted the grateful foster son, but 'I saw nothing' was a lie. You forced that lie on me."

"Zacharias, stop!" she shouts, "Stop!"

She twists in her seat.

"You let my father's body hang in the sun, rotting, for five days. You took me away and prevented me from helping my mother to bury him."

She stands up at last. I speak softly.

"Jesus Vasconcellos was your employee. You put him there. You must take responsibility for what he did, not only to my mother, but to the other women, too."

The door opens. Senhor Gavin is there with another man. He must be the new Consul.

"Miranda, dear, I thought I heard you call. Is something wrong?"

She turns away to hide her tears.

The Senhor smiles at the other man and speaks to him in English.

"This is the invaluable scribe and clerk I was telling you about. He will act as your interpreter until you have mastered Portuguese. Mr. Bates, may I present Zacharias Williams?"

Looking each man in the eye, I say, "That is not my name. I have been born again with the name my mother and my father gave me before I was baptized. My name is Kwame Zumbi."

"Kwame Zumbi, eh?" says Senhor Gavin. "Very pretty. Now tell me, Zacharias, who has given you the power to change your name? Mr. Bates, I hope I am not leaving you with a problem. This boy was christened Zacharias. I was (and am) his godfather. I honored him with the use of my own surname. His name will remain Zacharias Williams as long as he remains my property."

I look away, out of the window, down to the port where *The Love of Liberty* lies at anchor, one ship amongst many, some newly arrived slavers from Mina and Angola, others freighters loaded with the products of slave labor, bound for European ports.

I keep my counsel. Say what they will, my name is Kwame Zumbi. My name is Kwame Zumbi, and I will see to it, one day, that my daughter Nandzi Ama knows my mother Ama's story. I will see to it.

Glossary

Adowa, Akan: Asante dance

Akan, related West African peoples (including Asante and Fante) and their languages

allotment, market garden

Asante, Akan people of Ghana; their state; their language

asantehemaa, Akan: queen-mother of Asante; leading female royal (but note: not necessarily the mother of the Asantehene)

asantehene, Akan: king of Asante

Asase Yaa, Akan: female spirit of the earth (Thursday born)

awâwâwâ, **atúù**, Akan: greeting and reply of friends after a long separation

Bedagbam, Bekpokpam name for people of north eastern Ghana, more generally known as Dagomba

Bekpokpam, People of north eastern Ghana, more generally known as Konkomba; see also Kekpokpam

cachaça, Brazil: cheap rum distilled from sugar waste or molasses

cadeira, Brazil: curtained sedan chair

casa grande, Brazil: mansion, home of the senhor de engenho

cidade baixa, Brazil: lower city of Salvador

crioulo, Brazil: creole; African slave born in Brazil

Dagomba, people of north eastern Ghana, also known as Bedagbam

doek, head cloth

Elmina Castle, slave-trading castle built by the Portuguese at Edina on the coast of present-day Ghana in 1482-86

engenho, Brazil: sugar mill, or plantation

Engenho de Cima, Brazil: Upper Plantation

Engenho do Meio, Brazil: Middle Plantation

escravos, Brazil: slaves

Fante, West African Akan people; their states; their language

fontomfrom, Akan: talking drum

fogo morto, Brazil: derelict estate

Golden Stool, symbol of the unity of the Asante state

guinea corn, sorghum

Jesuits, Order of the Roman Catholic Church; one time slave owners, expelled from Brazil in 1759

Kekpokpam, area of north-eastern Ghana inhabited by a people who call themselves Bekpokpam (known to others as Konkomba; their language is Lekpokpam)

kòse, Akan: expression of sympathy; sorry

ladina, Brazil: female African born slave who has been baptized and who understands Portuguese

maakye, Akan: morning greeting; good morning (pronounce: maa-chi)

malungo, Brazil: slave who was a fellow-traveler on a slave ship

massapé, Brazil: heavy clay soil suitable for the cultivation of sugar

maté, Brazil: tea-like beverage

milréis, Brazil: old unit of currency

Mina, Brazil: the West African Gold Coast or Slave Coast

Misericórdia, Brazil: Charitable Brotherhood of the Holy House of Mercy

mma yeñkô, Akan: let's go

mónsoré, Akan: plural imperative of soré, get up

Na, title of Dagomba king

Palmares, Brazil: famous seventeenth century independent settlement of fugitive slaves

safra, Brazil: sugar harvest season

Sasabonsam, Akan: mythical ogre of the forest

senhor de engenho, Brazil: master of the sugar mill; owner of a sugar plantation

senzala, Brazil: slave cabin, hovel

shea-butter, fat made from seeds of the Shea tree, used as food, and for illumination, cosmetic purposes and making soap in West Africa

speculum oris, instrument shaped like a pair of scissors, used to force the mouth open

Tupi, people who lived in Bahia before the Portuguese colonized Brazil

vamos, Brazil: let's go

Ya Na, title of the Dagomba king

Yendi, the Dagomba capital

Zumbi, commanding officer of the army of Palmares

AUTHOR BIO

After taking a degree in Civil Engineering, Manu Herbstein left South Africa in 1959. He was twenty-three. He stayed away for thirty-three years, living and working in England and Scotland, India, Nigeria, and Zambia. He first worked in Ghana in 1961 and has lived there since 1970. Nowadays he visits his home town, Cape Town, at least once a year.

Manu Herbstein's novel, *Ama, a Story of the Atlantic Slave Trade,* won the 2002 Commonwealth Writers Prize for the Best First Book. The novel's companion website (http://www.ama.africatoday.com), won an Award for Innovative Use of New Media at the 2003 Highway Africa conference in South Africa.

Brave Music of a Distant Drum won an honorable mention in the 2010 Burt Award for Ghana, founded and funded by the Canadian philanthropist Bill Burt and administered by the Canadian Organization for Development through Education (CODE), through the Ghana Book Trust.